How could something that tasted so good hurt so bad?

As Hal Brognola flipped up the cap on the bottle of antacid tablets, several cascaded onto his lap, then onto the floor.

"Damn," he muttered, bending to pick them up. As he did, the plate-glass window shattered, chunks and splinters of glass sweeping across the table. The air blast of the round brushed against his scalp.

Brognola turned the bend into a shoulder roll. For a moment he lay stunned amid the broken glass, then his highly trained brain kicked in—two shots, one to break the glass, the second to kill. He had to move.

As the big Fed rolled away from the emptied windowframe, a bullet drilled into him, and everything went black. His momentum was just enough to carry him out of the line of fire.

Hal Brognola lay very still as a pool of blood spread from beneath his head.

MACK BOLAN ®

The Executioner

DON PENDLETON'S
THE EXECUTIONER®
SLAUGHTER SQUAD

A GOLD EAGLE BOOK FROM
WORLDWIDE®

TORONTO • NEW YORK • LONDON
AMSTERDAM • PARIS • SYDNEY • HAMBURG
STOCKHOLM • ATHENS • TOKYO • MILAN
MADRID • WARSAW • BUDAPEST • AUCKLAND

First edition March 1998
ISBN 0-373-64231-8

Special thanks and acknowledgment to
Alan Philipson for his contribution to this work.

SLAUGHTER SQUAD

We are warriors! Warriors all! We are going to kill a
mountain of terrorists!

> —From the Atlacatl Battalion song

My task is to separate the victims from the victimizers,
and in the process, the victimizers from their lives.

> —Mack Bolan

THE
MACK BOLAN®
LEGEND

Nothing less than a war could have fashioned the destiny of the man called Mack Bolan. Bolan earned the Executioner title in the jungle hell of Vietnam.

But this soldier also wore another name—Sergeant Mercy. He was so tagged because of the compassion he showed to wounded comrades-in-arms and Vietnamese civilians.

Mack Bolan's second tour of duty ended prematurely when he was given emergency leave to return home and bury his family, victims of the Mob. Then he declared a one-man war against the Mafia.

He confronted the Families head-on from coast to coast, and soon a hope of victory began to appear. But Bolan had broken society's every rule. That same society started gunning for this elusive warrior—to no avail.

So Bolan was offered amnesty to work within the system against terrorism. This time, as an employee of Uncle Sam, Bolan became Colonel John Phoenix. With a command center at Stony Man Farm in Virginia, he and his new allies—Able Team and Phoenix Force—waged relentless war on a new adversary: the KGB.

But when his one true love, April Rose, died at the hands of the Soviet terror machine, Bolan severed all ties with Establishment authority.

Now, after a lengthy lone-wolf struggle and much soul-searching, the Executioner has agreed to enter an "arm's-length" alliance with his government once more, reserving the right to pursue personal missions in his Everlasting War.

1

Morazán Province, El Salvador
December 15, 1992

The toll collector shoved his assault rifle–grenade launcher combo through the open window of the Toyota and pressed the muzzle of the M-16 A-1 against the driver's forehead. Slowly the coupe's doors swung open, and the male driver and a woman passenger got out, their empty hands in the air. The toll collector shouted at them, again poking his autorifle through the window. This time he aimed it at the car's rear seat. The woman half knelt, hands still raised, and quickly coaxed four small children, barefoot and dressed in dusty swimsuits, from the back of the vehicle. While the children hid behind her cotton dress, the toll collector searched the trunk and the engine compartment. Two other uniformed soldiers tore apart the inside of the car.

The Toyota's driver stole a quick glance over his shoulder at the stake truck, which, along with a pair of pickups, blocked the highway in both directions. A man in camo-flage fatigues and a boonie hat stood in the truck's bed, his hands on the fire controls of the .50-caliber Browning machine gun mounted on the roof of the cab. The weapon pinned the driver and his family where they had been herded, in the middle of the sweltering blacktop road.

Anything of value—a spare tire, tools, food, clothing—

was tossed in a pile on the ground by the three soldiers. The toll collector cleaned the driver's wallet of the few bills it contained and confiscated his well-polished dress shoes. Then, almost as an afterthought, he gun-butted the man in the face, just enough of a tap to break his nose. The children buried their heads in their mother's skirt, hiding from the sight of their father sitting on the road, cross-legged in his stocking feet, bright blood coursing from between his cupped hands.

Indifferent to the cruel little drama, trying to stay cool in the scant midafternoon shade, a dozen government-uniformed troops lay dozing in a grassy ditch alongside the road.

For them it was a rerun of a rerun.

FOUR HUNDRED YARDS uprange, Mack Bolan, a.k.a. the Executioner, lowered his armored binoculars and knuckled the strain from his eyes. After his vision cleared, he resumed his surveillance. The children were back in the car, and their father, his face concealed by a bloody handkerchief, slumped in the passenger seat. As the mother drove north, toward San Francisco de Gordoba, the toll collector waved forward the next vehicle in line.

Bolan backed off on the focus adjustments until he could see the waves of heat mirage shimmering off the blacktop. Satisfied that they were rising straight up from the roadway, that there was still no wind to compensate for, he turned the adjustments back to their premarked settings.

Behind him and to his right, deeper in the brush of the hillside hide, the two El Salvadoran military snipers quietly switched duties. The spotter took the sandbagged Heckler & Koch MSG-90 semiauto sniper rifle, and the shooter manned the 30 × 60 mm spotting scope. Their fatigues, like his, had no rank or insignia; like Bolan, they had no ID on their persons. If they got killed on this mission, they would be officially branded a rogue unit, operating in defiance of the already much violated cease-fire between the government and the Frente Martí Liberación Nacional—FMLN—guerrilla confederation.

Bolan watched the new shooter test the sheet of canvas spread out under the H&K's barrel with his palm. In the blistering heat its moisture had already evaporated. The sniper opened his canteen and resoaked the fabric. Wet canvas would smother the telltale dust cloud raised by the rifle's muzzle-blast and help conceal their position to counterfire. Attention to the small details kept a person alive.

As the shooter draped his leaf-decorated web veil over the rifle's action and Leupold ten-power telescopic sight, the guy behind the spotting scope heaved a big yawn. Tacho's upper front teeth looked like a row of broken bottle necks. The gruesome Halloween smile was the only way Bolan could tell Tacho and Gaspar, twins, apart. When the brothers and the other two-man sniper team had picked Bolan up at the Ilopango airport at midnight the night before, no last names had been exchanged. It was an economy measure. Why waste time memorizing lies? Any last names they offered would have been as false as the one on Bolan's own passport.

Although the five men had traveled with all their gear in a four-wheel-drive Suburban for several hours en route to the trailhead, little conversation was directed Bolan's way. Salsa music blared nonstop from the tape player, and when the El Salvadorans spoke, it was to one another, leaning close and employing short, rapid-fire bursts of local Spanish slang, which were usually followed by peals of coarse laughter. The four El Salvadorans had obviously worked together before.

Bolan didn't mind the lack of small talk or the fact that they pretended he didn't exist—that was something he expected, given his assignment. The tense, too eager joking around was no surprise to him, either; it reflected the extreme danger they were about to put themselves in.

The bantering ended when they parked at the rendezvous point, just outside the disputed territory of Morazán. The El Salvadorans were all business as they camo-painted one another's faces and strapped on day packs and weapons. With only the moonlight and jungle nightsong surrounding them, they moved cautiously up the narrow, twisting track. Bolan hung back, a distant rear guard with his over-under combination M-16 and 12-gauge riot pumpgun. He followed, a shadow of their shadows, evaluating the cross-country route they'd chosen, listening for their missteps and searching the backtrail for signs they had accidentally left behind, signs that betrayed their presence.

By the time they reached the kill zone, Bolan had no doubts about their fieldcraft. In the bush these guys knew what they were doing. And clearly they had learned something about tactics during their stay at Fort Benning's sniper school.

Thanks to the dense cover on either side of the highway, they could have stalked in and shot from less than one hundred yards, but they had selected their firing positions to take advantage of the range and accuracy of their weapons and to aid in a rapid, discreet retreat. The H&K MSG-90s the snipers carried were down-market versions of that manufacturer's top-of-the-line sniper weapon, the PSG-1. But they could still punch out three-quarter-inch groups of 7.62 mm Federal Match hollowpoints one hundred yards. That three-quarter minute of angle—MOA—accuracy translated into highly acceptable three-inch groups at four hundred yards.

The second two-man team, Rigo and Alphonso, had broken off from the column about three miles from the KZ and was now in position a half mile away on a low hill on the other side of the highway. The sniper units' fire lanes ran down both sides of the road, intersecting at the target. The cross fire and the echo effects of the narrow valley would confuse their opponents and complicate any attempt at pursuit. Retreat to the sniper teams' fallback positions would be quick and clean.

On paper it looked good.

The drone of a subsonic jet approaching from the south brought Bolan back to full alert. The roadblock crew heard it, too. For the third time since daybreak, they got real busy, real fast. The three trucks sped off the road, plunging single file down a crude, two-rut path under the canopy of trees. As the soldiers raced for cover after the trucks, they spread mats of fresh green leaves over the tire tracks leading into the bush.

When the El Salvadoran government Cessna A-37B buzzed the stretch of highway, the dust had drifted and dispersed over the treetops and there was nothing for the Dragonfly's minigun to shoot at. The civilian cars and trucks were all moving: from the air, it looked like a slow-poke in front was holding up the parade.

Ten minutes passed before the blockade re-formed and the process of exacting tribute began again.

Though the soldiers manning the roadblock wore government uniforms and carried government weapons, they were ERP, one of the five regional guerrilla movements that made up the FMLN. And the ERP was a cocky crew. It controlled most of Morazán, and had done so for decades despite the government's best efforts to wipe it out. Now, on the verge of peace, the ERP was about to take its place in the political arena of its nation. The occasional government air patrols were purely symbolic; they couldn't dent the ERP's fund-raising activities along the highway.

Even though the roadblock wasn't a government-sponsored operation, Bolan knew it could have been. Both sides in the civil war routinely indulged in beating, extortion, robbery, kidnap, rape, torture and summary execution. He wasn't in-country to decide which side did worse things to innocent citizens—that was a job for a historian. His assignment had nothing to do with the current conflict. He wasn't in-country to take lives, except if necessary in his own self-defense. He was in El Salvador as a favor to a friend, to observe and report on the technical aspects of the four-man sniper mission.

This day the Executioner was the judge.

From the north a dusty gray Nissan Pathfinder approached the barrier at high speed. It swerved to a stop in front of one of the pickup trucks, and four heavily armed men in uniform jumped out.

Showtime.

Bolan thumbed a foam sonic plug into his right ear, which was turned toward the H&K's muzzle, then scanned the four new arrivals with the binoculars. None of them wore insignia of rank, all appeared the same age and all wore sunglasses and khaki bill caps. The toll collector greeted the newcomers with open arms. He didn't salute any of them, so there was no telling which one was the head man.

Sweat burned in Bolan's eyes. He ignored it. The numbers were falling fast now. Once the cash pickup was completed, the Pathfinder and its occupants would be back up the road, and the store would be closed until tomorrow. If the sniper teams got jumpy and decided to target two of the four men at random, they only had a fifty-fifty chance of hitting the guerrilla commander. Taking the shot now would be a bad choice and would earn them an F.

It was so quiet in the hide that Bolan heard the breathing of the sniper shift into the slow, steady rhythm of the shoot cycle. His own breathing did the same, even though there were no cross hairs in the binocular's view field, even though his fingertip wasn't taking up the trigger's slack, then holding solid just before the breakpoint. Drops of sweat trickled down the sides of his face.

A third of a mile away, the toll collector reached into the baggy pocket of his fatigue pants and pulled out a doubled-over wad of bills four inches thick. He handed the money to the shortest soldier among the new arrivals.

He might as well have planted the kiss of death on his commander's cheeks, Mob style.

The H&K beside Bolan roared once, and a second later, from across the valley, he heard another gunshot.

Downrange the guerrilla leader was still smiling, clutching the money, when the first boattail hollowpoint hit him in the center of his chest. His teeth clenched, and his face twisted into a grimace as the sound of the first shot rolled over him. Then the second slug impacted, within an inch of the first, driving him backward. A mist of blood sprayed onto the men standing behind him, and the bills went flying as he slammed onto his back in the road. As the echoes of the shots mingled and the money floated down, the ERP leader quivered from head to foot.

It was nerve and muscle reflex. They had dropped him stone dead.

To make sure Bolan hadn't missed the outcome or its cause, Gaspar, the shooter, hissed in his direction, "Nailed that *terrorista* son of a bitch!"

Through the binoculars, the Executioner marked the looks of astonishment on the gore-spattered faces of the guerrillas, surprise that passed in a heartbeat. Then their autoweapons came up. They didn't return random answering fire, and they didn't duck for the cover of the roadside ditches. At a shouted command from the toll collector, the troops piled into the back of the stake truck and all three vehicles started down the road.

Gaspar let out a low moan. Both he and Tacho lay momentarily frozen, peering through their telescopes in disbelief as the trucks raced down the highway toward them.

Time to go.

"Move! ¡Ándale, pronto!" Bolan growled at the El Salvadorans. As Tacho and Gaspar scrambled up, Bolan caught the glint of something in the dirt at their feet. He scooped up the still-hot, spent shell case on the run and followed the two men down the trail.

Stealth no longer mattered. They crashed full tilt through the bush, trying to beat the trucks to the cutoff point, around the back side of the hill. Their line of retreat ran below the exposed ridge top, well inside the tree line. They had planned to put the summit between themselves and the enemy before crossing under cover to the far side of the hill and the trail that led back to the Suburban. On paper the sniper units' scheme had depended on concealment and on the ERP taking cover behind the roadblock—now it only depended on speed.

Whether the guerrillas had caught a muzzle-flash, a scope flash, whether they had been hit from the same positions before or whether they'd just gotten lucky, their response to hostile fire didn't surprise Bolan. The ERP was confident of its control of the territory and had no fear of falling into an ambush by government troops, who always operated with massive air and artillery cover and took few risks. Besides, the killing of an ERP commander would have enraged them.

The jungle trail twisted steeply down, and on the tight turns the soggy earth gave way under the pounding of their boots. Tacho tripped on a heavy root exposed by Gaspar and went sliding in the dirt. Bolan grabbed him by the belt and jerked him back to his feet.

For a split second they stared nose to nose. Fresh blood from a cut inside Tacho's mouth bubbled across his snaggleteeth. Then an earsplitting thunderclap rocked them to their boot heels. Orange flame blossomed in the tree canopy one hundred feet overhead. Bits of hot metal sang through the air, drilling into tree trunks and earth, severed branches and leaves raining on them.

Bolan shoved a cursing, blood-spitting Tacho ahead of him, through air thick with pulverized forest and corrosive smoke. Then the mounted Browning opened up from the middle of the highway. Fifty-caliber slugs swept through the jungle, clipping off more branches, leaves and vines. Another grenade blast lit up the canopy to the left. As they veered from the shrapnel spray, flame exploded in the treetops to their right.

In his mind's eye, Bolan could see the ERP lined up on both sides of the stake truck's bed, blindly firing 40 mm rifle grenades into opposing hillsides, walking the explosions deeper and deeper into the trees, hoping to wound them, to pin them down or to at least slow them so the pursuit could overtake them.

But the snipers didn't slow down. They pushed ahead, into the teeth of the bombardment. Gradually the booms outpaced them, then the explosions stopped.

The guerrillas had played their hand—they'd run out of high explosives, and the Browning could only saturate one side of the road at a time.

Without warning, Gaspar, the pointman, broke away from the trail, busting brush, cutting up the slope toward the tail of the ridge. Tacho turned after him, as if on cue.

Bolan paused on the path for a second, considering the sudden change of route. It looked like a panic turn, but there was no reason for the snipers to panic now. The grenade attack was over. They were well ahead of the ERP pursuit; the original retreat plan was still viable. In fact there was no way the guerrillas could catch them. They had an easy downhill glide back to the Suburban. They were home free, mission accomplished.

The Executioner took up the new route, following a cattle trail of broken branches and clear footprints the previously crafty El Salvadorans left in their wake. Even with the change of direction, they didn't have to leave clear signs; they had time enough to be careful.

That bothered him.

When Bolan caught up to them at the edge of the ridgeline clearing, Tacho and Gaspar had their day packs off and open. They didn't look worried. Tacho gestured for Bolan to go ahead and cross the short stretch of open ground to the other side of the ridge. The Executioner scanned the tree line for movement and human shape among the shadows and, seeing none, took a dozen steps into the bright sunlight. Then, crouching low, he glanced back to make sure the El Salvadoran snipers were coming. They weren't. Tacho and Gaspar had their backs to him and, as he watched, each tossed three hand-sized objects into the jungle.

A chorus of metallic snapping sounds came from inside the tree line. Squinting, Bolan caught the glint of the monofilament trigger lines as they shot like spiderwebs twenty feet in all directions, disappearing as they draped over the freshly broken trail, the low limbs and bushes.

Though their limited mission was complete and they were no longer in danger, though their explicit orders were to make the hit and to withdraw without further contact, the environment remained target rich for the snipers. Whether those targets were legitimate under the circumstances—or whether this was simply a bit of recreational murder—it was too late for Bolan to do anything about it.

With six antipersonnel mines laid and armed, the trap was neatly set. No matter how cautiously the ERP dogged the snipers' apparently terror-driven retreat, when the guerrillas saw the clearing coming up ahead, they were bound to close ranks for a short distance, to pause while they decided how to deal with the stretch of open ground and a potential ambush from the dense tree line on the other side.

Bunched up was exactly how Tacho and Gaspar wanted them.

In a free-fire zone, Bolan thought grimly, only one thing was certain: shit happened. And it was about to happen to the ERP.

The Executioner walked on.

They were a good three-quarters of a mile down the trail when a pop like a firecracker came from the hilltop, followed a half second later by a solid thundercrack. Tacho and Gaspar stopped jogging and listened. Almost at once, a string of crackles resounded from the ridge, the noise abruptly overlaid by jumbled, rolling thunder.

Bolan walked around the high-fiving snipers and continued down the trail. He was familiar with the antipersonnel mines they had used. Like the "Bouncing Betty," the newer M-86 Pursuit Deterrent Munition had a johnny-jump-up feature: the monofilament trip lines triggered a small explosive charge that raised the one-pound mine to belly height, at which point the main charge detonated.

Vultures would soon be pecking the eyes out of the mangled ERP survivors, those unlucky enough to still have eyes.

On the ride back to San Salvador, the two sniper teams no longer attempted to conceal their conversation from him, perhaps because they figured they had passed the test with flying colors, perhaps because they had mistakenly read his bleak silence as approval.

"I shot first," Gaspar boasted. "The kill is mine."

The tall one called Rigo, who was driving the Suburban, corrected him. "You shot second...and missed."

"I always shoot first and always make the hit. You shoot slow and sloppy, like an old woman with shaky hands."

The taunts went back and forth for several minutes, with no resolution and growing hostility between the shooters. Before things got out of hand, Rigo's partner, Alphonso, changed the subject. "Did you see the target's face when he took the bullet?" Alphonso screwed up his round, dimpled face in a crude parody of the guerrilla leader's death agony, causing the others to hoot with laughter. He turned toward Bolan to share the fun.

The Executioner stared into his eyes, and Alphonso's playacted pain was suddenly real. Returning the tall American's gaze, the El Salvadoran had a disturbing vision that came and went in a sudden flash like a chain-lightning strike. He saw row upon row of unmarked tombstones, neat, white and hard like teeth jutting up from a grassy field; they stretched all the way to the horizon and a swirling sky the color of bullet lead. The vision was so oppressive it made his mouth go dry and his throat ache.

"Música, por favor," Bolan said.

Alphonso broke the stranglehold of those hard blue eyes and cued up the tape player. Salsa again blared from the Suburban's sound system, drowning out most of the sniper teams' small talk.

Though Bolan tried to concentrate on the music, certain repeated words and phrases, mostly meaningless to him, crept into his consciousness, as did the general topic of discussion. The El Salvadorans were bragging to one another about sex and killing. To Bolan it sounded like the sex and the killing were connected, as in simultaneous acts, as in rape-murder.

According to what he'd been told at the premission briefing, these snipers were disciplined, highly professional soldiers. After working with them for fourteen hours, after adding up the bits and pieces of circumstantial evidence, he strongly suspected they were something much less.

Now, in the confines of the Suburban, they seemed to give off the familiar reek of mobster, of terrorist, of death squad.

How close to death were the snipers as they traded their stories of carnal butchery? All that separated them from hell's terrifying gate was the Executioner's word of honor to a friend. Because of the unique situation, he wasn't free to pursue the matter as he normally would have: verification, termination.

When Rigo stopped the Suburban in front of the Holiday Inn, Bolan got out without a word. He didn't look back.

In the loose-fitting slacks and sport shirt he had changed into, Bolan easily passed for the industrial consultant his entry visa claimed he was. As he rounded the central courtyard's swimming pool, a flock of minimally swimsuited women looked up from their jumbo umbrella drinks with undisguised interest, which he didn't acknowledge.

Hal Brognola rose from his chair beside the hotel's loudly splashing fountain and extended his hand in greeting. "Mack, good to see you. Make yourself at home."

The Executioner took a seat across the table from him, setting his carryon at his feet. Almost at once, they were set upon by a uniformed waiter. Bolan waved the man away. "Nothing for me."

Brognola waited until the man had gone, then asked, "How'd it go?"

"The job's done."

"How did the new employees work out?"

"No complaints about their technical abilities. They know the field, they can plan and they can shoot."

"So, they have your stamp of approval?"

"Negative."

"What happened?"

"I have a bad feeling about these guys. They went beyond the specific limits of the assignment," Bolan said. "And they enjoy the wet work too much to suit me." In terse, clinical detail he explained the events that had taken place earlier in the day.

"Maybe they had a score to settle," the man from the Justice Department countered. "Lots of grudges can spring up in twenty years of civil war. Or maybe it was some kind of macho Central American thing. You've got to remember we're coming from different cultures here. Or maybe they just thought it would impress you."

"It did impress me," Bolan said. "You never showed me their service histories. You got them?"

"Yeah."

"Who gave them to you?"

"El Salvador military."

"And you believe what's in them?"

"All I can say is this operation has nothing to do with ES. The military has no reason to lie to us."

"Except that's what they do best." Bolan looked into Brognola's eyes and knew that his friend was withholding information and concealing his own personal opinion. He respected the big Fed's sworn obligation to do just that, and didn't press. On this job the Executioner knew only what he needed to know, nothing more.

Brognola fumbled in his shirt pocket and removed a half-dozen antacid tablets. He ate them all without counting or even looking at them, then washed down the chalky grit with a gulp of ice water. "Bottom line is," he said, clearing his throat, "are these guys good enough to freelance out of country?"

"I wouldn't have them on any team of mine."

"That's not a consideration—they aren't being recruited for your team," Brognola assured him. "I need a direct answer from you. Can these guys do the work?"

"Like I said, on the technical end they check out." Bolan pushed his chair back from the table. "Sounds to me like you've already made up your mind to sign them on.

You're an old hand, Hal. I know you can handle whatever heat comes your way. Will you take some friendly advice, though?''

"From you, always."

Bolan leaned across the table. "Keep a tight rein on these guys," he stated, modulating his voice so the big Fed could just hear it over the sound of the fountain. "Don't give them more firepower than they need for their assignment. And the first time they screw up, yank them."

Both men rose. "Thanks for the favor, Mack," Brognola said. "This one was beyond the call."

"Between us, nothing's ever beyond the call, pal. Got a plane to catch."

BROGNOLA SAT AWHILE after the big man left, absently gnawing an unlit cigar. He was delaying his return to suite 235 and a reconvening of the supersecret oversight panel known simply as R.

There was no qualifying adjective in front of the single letter, no group or operation designation that a random computer search could key on, no clue as to what or why or who R might be. Good thing, too, because in philosophy and deed, R ran counter to the terms of the Geneva Convention, and violated both U.S. and international law—specifically Article 15 of the Charter of the Organization of American States: "No state or group of states has the right to intervene, directly or indirectly, for any reason whatever, in the internal or external affairs of any other state."

R was a no-prisoners-no-borders campaign in the War on Drugs, and it had the potential of being the proverbial dead rat on the kitchen floor of the White House.

Count on Bolan to hit the soft spot, Brognola thought, clenching the cigar butt between his teeth. For all practical purposes, the decision *had* been made. Getting the snipers vetted by an expert outside the usual military-intelligence community channels was the final, low hurdle that needed jumping. The El Salvadorans were on board—even if under their squeaky-clean dossiers they turned out to be nothing but a bunch of death-squad hack-and-chop boys.

Brognola wished he could've laid the whole thing out for his longtime friend, but that was out of the question. He never believed the sniper angle would further R's mission, and he didn't trust El Salvadoran brass or its slick liaison, Lieutenant-Colonel Rudolfo Suarez. But the final call wasn't his. It was a team decision. In this case, democracy misapplied—it all boiled down to politics and turf control in the labyrinth of D.C.

No point putting this off any longer, he told himself. As he got up, Brognola fumbled in his shirt pocket for more antacid tabs. His fingertips found only lint and white dust. He knew he had to stop by his room on the way and stock up, because he sure as hell was going to need them.

"THE ES SHOOTERS ARE a go," Brognola said to the group of seven men and one woman seated around suite 235's conference table. "I know I'm outvoted here, but before we activate them I want to state my objections to this part of the plan, for the record."

The two agents from the CIA—one black, the other white, with identical buzz cuts and tropical-weight suits— traded put-upon, give-me-a-break looks. Colonel Suarez appeared mildly amused at the prospect. As Brognola started ticking off the sniper campaign's potential problems, the El Salvadoran liaison brushed imaginary dust from the bright brass buttons of his impeccably tailored officer's jacket.

"First of all, it's unreasonable to expect to control untested field operatives at such long distance," Brognola said. "Once these men are in place, it's going to be difficult or impossible to withdraw them because they're their own masters—independent operatives seeking targets of opportunity. Because no in-country support apparatus exists, their long-term survival is doubtful. Any escape and evasion is going to be up to them. If they're caught by the opposition or the opposition's hirelings in the police or military, it could jeopardize security on our larger mission. In my opinion, the risk just isn't worth taking. After all, we're only talking about a minimal increase in the irritation factor here. This is a very small part of the overall operation. It could be sacrificed without losing anything.''

"You're ignoring the cumulative psychological effects of this type of ongoing harassment,'' Bob Sutro said. The CIA man was an expert on sublethal-lethal psychological operations, as was his partner, Dick Albright. Together they had coauthored several widely circulated Agency monographs on the subject. Brognola knew that successful careers had been built on considerably less. Though their territory was well staked out, it still needed occasional watering—with blood.

Albright finished Sutro's thought for him, like the other half of an old married couple. "Even if the snipers only manage to terminate middle-level traffickers,'' he said, "it's bound to demoralize the Medellín command-in-control structure. No one has ever challenged them like this before. They'll be angry and they'll be spooked. And their attention will be diverted from the broader and deeper lines of attack we're taking.''

"It'll put the fear of God into those arrogant bastards,'' Sutro said with conviction.

Brognola could see they were all buying it: the DEA reps, Ed Hartwell and Dan Freeberg; Brognola's counterpart from DAS—the Colombian equivalent of the FBI—Augustin Murillo; and the man and woman from the State Department, Ken Patachi and Eleanor McCullen. The only unsmiling face at the table belonged to the man from the El Salvadoran military.

"Mr. Brognola, I deeply resent your implication that these El Salvadoran soldiers are not professional enough to handle the assignment," Colonel Suarez said. "I suggest you reread their service records carefully. They have been operating independently for many years, living off the land and their own wits deep inside enemy-held territory. These are dedicated, self-sacrificing heroes of the anti-communist struggle and the fight for democracy in my country. They are the best of our best. If you send them in to kill members of the Medellín cartel, that's what they'll do until you recall them."

The colonel was good, but even he couldn't maintain a stone face. Beneath his pencil mustache, a flicker of a grin twisted his lips. He'd already won, and he knew that Brognola knew it.

"If we don't see the names of the dead cartel members in the Bogotá papers," Hartwell from DEA added, "we don't authorize funds to the Bogotá banks. If the snipers don't perform, they don't get paid. There's no control problem here, Hal."

Brognola addressed the Colombian agent. "And you don't have any difficulty with that from a professional standpoint?"

"If my superiors at DAS thought they could handle the Medellín cartel by themselves, using conventional means," Augustin Murillo said, "believe me, I wouldn't be sitting here talking to you."

"I think a majority of us agree that the snipers should proceed without further delay," Eleanor McCullen said.

Brognola looked around the table. Each of them had a private cow to milk, a part of the whopping big plan that was theirs alone. The pair from State wanted the Colombian army and DAS to kidnap cartel leaders and ship them to the U.S. for trial. The DEA boys wanted to seize or destroy cartel assets *inside* Colombia, using U.S. air strikes if necessary. The DAS wanted the cartel gone so badly that the hiring of foreign assassins didn't faze them. And they were all willing to trade support for support. Brognola knew this was how the game was played. Whether R succeeded in eliminating the cartel or not, his task was to keep the snipers from turning into an embarrassment for the White House.

These folks weren't going to make the job easy for him.

Feeling a sudden twinge, Brognola started for his stomach medicine. He stopped when he realized that Suarez was watching him closely, in fact was gleefully awaiting the now familiar movement, the fingers dipping into the shirt pocket, the external sign of his internal pain.

Instead of the fat white tabs, Brognola took out a pen. Then he winked at the El Salvadoran.

2

Valle Province, Colombia
February 2, 1993

In the Leupold Ultra's ten-power view field, a great orange-and-black-striped beast paced back and forth, pounding out time like a metronome.

Tacho Ruiz wiped the sweat from his hands. He hadn't been so excited over a shot in a long time—until this moment he had only dreamed of bagging a tiger.

He cautioned himself to calm down as he turned the scope on an empty fifty-five-gallon oil drum that stood outside the barless zoo enclosure and served as a trash can. Using the scope's Mil Dot reticle, he figured the range to his target. The drum's height was standard, so all he had to do was measure it against the scale of little dots overlaying the vertical Duplex cross hair. He did some quick division in his head and got a distance of 650 yards. He clicked in the yardage with the scope's Bullet Drop Compensator—BDC—knob, which zeroed the scope internally, according to the characteristics of the Match-grade 7.62 mm bullet he was using. Thanks to the BDC, instead of raising or lowering the aim point to correct for the bullet's ballistics at the target distance, Tacho could now take the shot with the cross hairs dead-on.

The Bengal tiger moved inside its landscaped prison as if it had a counter in its head, ticking off the laps. It did eight back and forths, then paused one second before making the turn that started the cycle over again. Tacho held the scope steady and let the tiger do the work.

Bing! Mentally he squeezed off a round as the animal hesitated, then he counted the beats until it walked into the path of the imaginary .308 boattail hollowpoint. Good. He repeated the procedure, this time adjusting his Mil Dot lead for the light wind at the target. Bing! He tracked his make-believe 168-grain slug straight through the big cat's lungs.

Gaspar, who was manning the spotter scope, lightly touched his brother's shoulder. "The Turkey is coming, Tacho," he said. He pointed across the broad green valley to the angular slabs of glitter-flecked concrete, the huge smoked-glass windows of the ultramodern white palace built on the isolated hill overlooking the private zoo.

The drug lord's mansion was protected by its elevation and by the twenty-foot-high concrete wall that encircled its grounds. The private zoo had no elevation to speak of, and its security wall was still under construction. From their position on the side of a slightly higher hill across the valley, Gaspar and Tacho watched a group of men stroll down the winding gravel path that led from the mansion's side gate to the zoo. Three of the men were armed: two had mini-Uzis and one had a Kalashnikov AKM. The fourth guy carried a five-gallon plastic bucket by the wire handle. The last of the walkers was an overweight man dressed in a white silk suit and a broad-brimmed white planter's hat— Gilberto "the Turkey" Chunchullo.

Tacho tracked the drug lord and his crew as they passed enclosures housing various rare and endangered animals. The entourage stopped when they reached the tiger.

As Gilberto Chunchullo mopped his shiny face with a huge white handkerchief, Tacho laid the Duplex cross hairs on his vast, soft belly. Some fat men wore their belts below their stomachs, so they could pretend they still had thirty-two-inch waists—not so, the Turkey. His belt proudly rode the maximum circumference, the equator.

The man carrying the bucket approached the drug lord and offered it to him. Chunchullo donned an orange rubber gauntlet to protect his snow-white sleeve, then reached into the bucket and withdrew a chunk of raw meat. Leaning against the enclosure wall, he waggled the two-pound slab in the tiger's direction. The big cat paid no attention to the man or the beef, but kept on pacing back and forth, back and forth.

Tacho swung his aim point away from Chunchullo, lining up the Duplex's horizontal cross hair with the path of the tiger.

"WHAT'S WRONG with him?" Chunchullo demanded of his underlings. "Why won't he eat?"

They shrugged; they had no answers. They were just bodyguards.

He threw the prime beef back into the bucket and tore off the rubber gauntlet. The tiger had refused all food since its arrival the week before, and now Chunchullo was afraid it might be sick. He had a guarantee of good health from the dealer in rare and illicit animals, but even if he chose to exchange the beast for another, he couldn't recoup the considerable transportation and palm-greasing costs for this one. The drug lord didn't have to worry about money. He was one of the one hundred richest men in the world. He *liked* to worry about money.

Chunchullo considered himself a wise and canny businessman, and in a twisted way, he was. Certainly wiser than his competition from the north, the Medellín cartel which answered every problem with murder or threats of murder. There was no future in a brute-force approach.

Like the other top members of the Cali cocaine cartel, Chunchullo used his head, applying the carrot instead of the stick, silver instead of lead whenever possible. The members of the Cali organization had taken another lead from the American Mafia and worked hard to diversify their enterprises. They had become their country's major landowners; they had used coca profits to buy their way into legitimate business and all levels of politics and the military. They were known as the "good drug lords." Like their Medellín counterparts, Cali members had a public image to maintain. Image was what Chunchullo's private zoo was really all about. It was the height of extravagance, of decorative spending, both a symbol and a demonstration of his vast financial power.

The drug lord spoke to the man on his left, his number one. "Arturo, take the small helicopter and find my veterinarian. I don't care where he is or what he's doing. Bring him to me at once. No excuses from—"

Suddenly the pacing tiger staggered in midstride, its front legs half-buckling, its chest nearly dropping to touch the well-packed earth. The sound of the distant gunshot was nearly lost in the tiger's roar of pain. Even though Chunchullo was looking right at the cat, it took his brain long seconds to comprehend what had just happened. The mortally wounded beast leaped ten feet in the air, twisting, slashing out blindly with its claws while gore jetted from its throat.

A second gunshot rolled over them.

On the drug lord's right, the man holding the meat bucket sagged. A ragged star-shaped second mouth had opened up in the front of his neck. He toppled to the ground without a sound.

Arturo shoved Chunchullo ahead of him, forcing him down behind the low wall that supported the hurricane fence of the emu's quarters. The drug lord peeked over the wall as the crack of the gun shot reached them. The big, flightless bird lay on its back in a cloud of dust, an enormous hole in the side of its body, its long legs feebly kicking in the air.

"My animals! What is going on?" Chunchullo growled.

"There are two shooters, boss," Arturo said. "They're toying with us. Probably Medellín mercenaries. They're a long way off, but they have the angle on us and they have the range. We've got to move. We've got to get back to the big house and solid cover."

"Okay, okay," Chunchullo said. "Let's do it."

The drug lord couldn't run uphill very fast, so he ordered two of his guards to follow closely, shielding him from a shot in the back. They had traveled less than fifty feet before both men were hit, one guard shot through the lower spine from the rear, the other taking a bullet from the side.

As Chunchullo reached the bear's enclosure, it, too, died before his eyes. Reared up on its hind legs, it was an easy target. He saw the backlit puff of dust explode from the fur between its eyes. The animal crashed to earth, one thousand pounds of deadweight.

"Don't stop!" Arturo said, grabbing his arm. "Don't stop! Keep going!"

With Arturo pushing him from behind, Chunchullo managed to scramble over the top of the low rock wall that secured the rhino pit. His outstretched arms weren't strong enough to break his face-first fall. Another gunshot echoed as he landed in something warm and squishy, something that smelled awful. He looked up to see the baby rhino staring at him. It was so little that it was concealed from gunfire by the wall. Then he realized that his number one hadn't followed him.

"Arturo!"

No answer.

Arturo hadn't made it.

"Anybody! Help! Get me out of here!"

No answer.

As he crouched behind the wall, Chunchullo's mind raced. No help was going to come. The rest of his crew up in the mansion wouldn't think anything of a few single gun shots from across the valley; they wouldn't come running. And he couldn't go to them because he was too slow. He really had only one option: he could stay behind the wall and wait for the killers to come for him.

Then something occurred to him. Although the snipers had slaughtered everyone around him, even his animals, they hadn't taken a shot at him. And they certainly could have done so any number of times. Maybe they had never intended to kill him. Maybe all this was just supposed to scare him. Maybe the Medellín cartel wanted him alive, to take the news back to his Cali partners that they could do this to any of them, any time they wanted.

If it would save his life, Chunchullo had no problem with being a messenger boy for the Devil himself.

RIGO HELD HIS CROSS HAIRS trained on the top of the wall where the fat man had gone over and waited for the tap from Alphonso. His spotter wasn't only marking bullet impacts for him but he was also timing the shots, making sure that he fired no more than one round every two minutes, allowing the H&K MSG-90's barrel to cool down. The sniper rifle had been sighted in with a cold barrel, zeroed for a one-shot kill. To maintain bench-rest accuracy in combat, they had to keep the barrel's temperature low.

And Rigo's accuracy this day had proved almost uncanny. He was on top of his form, confident in his weapon and his control of the distance to target. For that reason, when Chunchullo rose from behind the wall, waving his white hat in one hand and a big white hanky in the other, he didn't take the easy torso shot. Instead, he targeted the neural strip just above the man's left ear.

When Alphonso touched his elbow, Rigo let it rip. He

rode the recoil wave and recovered the target through the scope just as the drug lord's head exploded in a pink cloud. Chunchullo dropped from view, behind the wall.

Then Rigo killed the baby rhino.

"Too bad we have to leave them all behind," Alphonso said, scanning the murdered zoo animals with the spotting scope.

Rigo knew his partner wasn't lamenting the loss of valuable horn or the various rare glands prized in Oriental medicine; he wasn't even thinking about what they could get for the animal skins. He was thinking about the powerful *sopa del estrago,* slaughterhouse soup, that they could've made of the pelts, guts, bone, feathers, blood and meat of the dead creatures. A flood of memories descended upon Rigo, memories of *matanzas,* the glorious mass killings of the past.

As part of the notorious Atlacatl Battalion of the El Salvadoran army, he, Alphonso, Gaspar, Tacho had swept across the disputed sectors of El Salvador like a plague of black-helmeted locusts, destroying everything in sight. At night, as an initiation ritual for new recruits, they had collected the corpses of farm and wild animals they had shot or roadkilled and cooked them, pelts and all, in huge open caldrons. The brave soldiers of the Atlacatl had howled at the stars between gulps of that boiling, bloody stew. Only they dared to drink it, they who were the most manly of men, whose courage put all other men to shame.

It was the creed of the Atlacatl Battalion that black deeds of great virility tempered the heart, forged the spirit and bonded warriors forever as brothers. A fellow former Atlacatl, an officer, had landed them the Colombian assignment. Though nothing had been said directly, the understanding was that once in-country, the snipers were free to balance loyalty to their unnamed employers with their own self-interest. Atlacatl alumni never let the former interfere with the latter. They trusted each other in one area only. They were sworn to forgive anything of their own, and to protect them, no matter their crimes.

Once in-country, it was only natural that the snipers migrate to the Medellín cartel, which specialized in murder and acts of terror, and paid their assassins by the head for their enemies. The Cali side, on the other hand, was made up of despicable bean counters like Chunchullo.

Rigo surveyed their handiwork through the telescopic sight a last time. They had left a potent message for the men they had been sent to Colombia to exterminate.

Illustrated by Cali blood and brains, the message was, "If you like what you see, make us an offer."

3

Washington, D.C.,
The Present

Ken Patachi hung his head out the open driver's window. He could see taillights flashing way past the Duke Street overpass. A construction delay on the interstate had the late-Friday-afternoon traffic stopped dead. Somewhere ahead everything funneled down to one lane to make room for the road crew's equipment. There wasn't supposed to be any construction going on during peak traffic, which was brutal enough all by itself. It had to be an emergency repair, Patachi thought.

Since he hadn't moved an inch in ten minutes, he decided to turn off the Buick's engine to save gas. In the windows of the high-rises overlooking the sunken section of highway, he could see people moving around. They were the smart ones. They didn't commute.

The brake lights ahead of him winked off, and the line of cars started moving forward at a snail's pace. Patachi had advanced about half a block when he saw the woman holding the Slow sign. He was ten cars away, nine, eight, seven. He tried to communicate with her telepathically, pleading with her not to turn it.

As he crept up to her, he heard the squawk of her radio and knew he wasn't going to make it. Sure enough, she swiveled the sign to the red side.

The woman smiled at the driver in the car in front of him.

He shut off his engine again and considered the advantages of her job as opposed to his. There was no margin for error in her profession, no frustrating shades of gray. It was either Stop or Slow. Red or orange. She got lunch breaks, snack breaks and plenty of open, if not fresh, air. He wondered what her retirement plan was like. Lately he had been thinking about retirement, thinking that he never wanted to do it. He considered himself the kind of guy who died pulling in harness. He was hooked on the pressure, and he enjoyed being in the presence of real power, even if the controls weren't usually in his hands. At one time he thought he might leave the State Department and go into teaching at some small eastern college; now he wasn't so sure he had the patience for it. Kids today were a mess. Hell, adults today were a mess.

His cellular phone chirped.

"Ken here," he said.

"How you doin'?"

The unfamiliar voice had a thick Spanish accent.

"Who is this?"

"A friend..."

"What number are you calling?"

"Yours, Mr. Patachi."

"What do you want?"

"Just to talk while you're stopped in traffic."

Patachi looked around to see if someone close was using a car phone. Negative. But it had to be some kind of practical joke. He hated practical jokes. "Play your dumb game with somebody else, Junior. I don't have time for it."

"That's right. You got no more time. In fact, your time is up."

"Stick it, jerk," Patachi said.

Before he could hit the phone's disconnect button, something drilled through the open window and slammed him low in the side of the neck. It was the hardest single punch he had ever taken, or would ever take. It knocked him unconscious. He came to almost at once, instinctively fighting back the waves of blackness and nausea. His whole body was numb, and he was suddenly so weak he could barely draw breath. The seat belt's shoulder harness was all that was holding him up.

Then he saw the blood and realized he'd just been shot. Swallowing the fear, he tried to hang up the phone so he could call 911. It was then he discovered he couldn't move.

Patachi was no stranger to bullet wounds. He had seen men shot many times. He could visualize the downward angle of the bullet track and knew it had to have clipped his spinal cord. He was paralyzed. "Oh, fuck," he groaned. "Oh, fuck."

"He said something. He's still alive."

The words came from the car phone's speaker. Electricity crab-crawled under his scalp.

If Patachi could've reached the sun visor, he could've grabbed the Tactical One-Hander knife he kept there. With its serrated blade, he could've slashed through the seat belts in a second. Freed of the restraint, he could've dropped down, out of the firing lane. But Patachi couldn't raise his arm from his lap.

He knew what was coming next. The second bullet was the ice-cold hammer.

It hit him below the earlobe, at the point of the jaw. The mushrooming slug went through and through, exiting his head and blowing out the passenger window.

The crash of glass made the sign woman turn to look. She couldn't see into the front seat of the Buick anymore. The inside of its windshield was fogged with red.

ED HARTWELL SAT in the deep shade, sipping iced tea, watching the rest of his family play doubles badminton in the sunshine in the park's broad playing field. He was pleased at what he saw. Both he and his wife, Kate, were highly competitive. They had worked hard to instill the urge to succeed in their three children. Maybe, he thought, Kate was regretting that just a little bit now as she battled their oldest son, Matthew, tooth and nail for a tie-breaking point.

He and Kate set aside Saturday midday for family time. Their kids were still young enough that they didn't prefer to be off with their friends on the weekends. That wouldn't last much longer. This Saturday it was a picnic in the public park with a round-robin badminton tournament. The winner would escape all normally assigned household chores for one week.

"Yes!" Matt shouted as his mother failed to reach his powerhouse smash.

"Nice shot," Kate said, wiping her forehead with the terry-cloth sweatband on her wrist. She looked at her husband and grinned.

As she stood, bent forward and tensed, awaiting her oldest son's serve, Hartwell thought how great she looked in shorts, how much he still desired her. In the next instant she just crumpled. Kate hit the ground rag-doll limp, making no attempt to protect her face. His mind dimly registered a car's backfire in the distance, but Hartwell didn't connect the sound with the event. His first thought was that his wife had had a stroke or a heart attack. His own heart pounding with dread, he ran from the deeply shaded picnic bench to her side. When he turned her over on her back, he saw spreading red from an exit wound in the middle of her chest.

"Oh, God, Kate," he said. One look had told him that she was dead, and in that same instant he knew that this horrible thing was connected to his job at DEA, that it was his fault, that he had put the ones he loved the most in mortal danger. Instinctively he looked up, searching the far edge of the playing field for the source of the shot. They had killed her to draw him out of the shadows and away from the cover of the coolers and boxes on the picnic table.

And it had worked.

He was crouching, off balance when the single bullet hit him. It bowled him over onto his back. Paralyzed by the massive shock, he could feel the blood pouring out of his chest, the pain drilling into his very core. He could hear his kids screaming above him. He tried to tell them to get down, but his voice wouldn't work. There was nothing he could do to protect them. Nothing ever again.

The family dog frantically nuzzled the side of his face—cold nose, warm tongue at his ear. The feeling gradually faded as life slipped away.

HALFWAY THROUGH his meal, Hal Brognola was slowing down. He wasn't full yet, but he was nearly there.

"And how is your chicken tonight?" his waiter asked.

"Excellent, as always," Brognola said. "My compliments to Mr. Santangelo."

Brognola sat back in his chair and sipped at a glass of wine. On the other side of the plate-glass window, traffic was light on the broad avenue. This was one of his favorite restaurants, one of the few that knew how to make a fresh marinara sauce. As an added plus, it wasn't far from his office.

Because of the Patachi murder the evening before, he had missed both breakfast and lunch. He was grabbing a quick early dinner so he could work all night again tonight. His wife understood. Weekends meant nothing when a friend and colleague was gunned down.

The first question was whether the killing was a random act of violence: some lone gun settling a score with the world in general and no one in particular. That had been quickly resolved by the initial crime-scene investigation. Patachi had been shot twice, by two different .308-caliber weapons. From the angles of the bullet strikes, the CID people put the snipers' hides in the lower stories of a high-rise apartment building overlooking the highway. A search of the lower floors had turned up two firing locations, separated by 150 feet of corridor—enough distance to give the shooters firing lanes that crossed in the middle of the interstate, some two hundred yards away.

It added up only one way: an execution-style hit with the man from State as the designated target.

From a couple of hundred yards out, with little or no elevation angle to compensate for, and a stationary target, it would have been an easy-money shot for an average marksman using optical sights on a decent deer gun. In other words, the killers or whoever hired them could have been anybody with a bone to pick with Patachi.

Brognola was running searches of all of Patachi's assignments, starting from the most recent and working backward. The man had had an interesting professional life, which made the task more difficult. A whole lot of very bad people had good reason to wish him ill. His murderers could have had U.S. or overseas organized-crime connections. They could have been terrorists or Communists. The big Fed figured he was probably going to have to unravel Patachi's whole career to get a handle on it.

He'd had a report from a mutual friend at the State Department that Patachi's wife, Mitzy, was falling apart, that she was under heavy sedation. No point in calling her yet. He'd wait a day or so, maybe go by in person. It wasn't something he was looking forward to.

Brognola raised his glass, silently toasting his departed friend and pledging him swift justice, if not revenge. He refilled the glass from the bottle at his left hand.

The thing that both puzzled and irked him was that apparently Patachi always took the same route home in the same car. A guy with his experience should have known better. All somebody had to do was to wait outside his office and call the snipers when he left the parking lot. The finger man might have followed him onto the highway to make sure, but that wasn't absolutely necessary. Sooner or later Patachi had to drive right under the killers' guns.

Brognola sliced off another piece of chicken breast and speared it with his fork. It was so easy to get overconfident, to forget that the other side had all the time in the world, that they could afford to wait for the right moment to strike.

He was just as guilty as Patachi in that regard.

But that hadn't occurred to him yet.

GASPAR RUIZ PULLED BACK from the sniper rifle's scope. As he did so, the sharp grit of the roofing compound dug through his shirtsleeves into his elbows. "That glass looks thick," he advised his brother. "It will deflect the bullet. We might only wound him. We might miss him altogether. Maybe we should wait until he steps out the front door."

Tacho didn't have to think about it. "No. He's sitting there for us like a paper target. We're both going to shoot. I'll break the glass with my bullet, and you follow up with the kill shot."

Gaspar watched as Tacho picked up his Springfield Armory M-1 A National Match rifle and found the stockweld with his cheek, positioning his eye the proper distance from the scope's ocular lens. Tacho released the safety and started his slow, even shoot-cycle breathing.

The distance to target was short, shorter even than for the man on the interstate. But what with the recoil of their weapons and the distraction of the falling glass, they might not be able to tell if they had taken their man out. That there'd be no spotter on this hit concerned Gaspar, but not overly so. They had practiced this same routine many times on the firing range and had used it in Colombia to take out a rare and endangered species there—an incorruptible judge. They had shot him in the head as he stood rinsing a cup in front of his kitchen sink. The timing between the two shots was critical. There couldn't be enough of a gap to allow a flinch or a duck from the target, but there had to be enough time to allow the windowpane to fully implode.

Gaspar snuggled up to the H&K MSG-90, seating the adjustable buttstock against his shoulder. One good thing about having a twin for a partner was that he and Tacho could trade guns back and forth without having to worry about differences in stock fit. With the scope's BDC set at two hundred yards, Gaspar had to hold a little low to compensate for the bullet's rise over the shorter distance. Reaching under his armpit, he made the necessary adjustment by gently squeezing the bean bag positioned under the rifle butt.

Though he put the cross hairs slightly below the earlobe, the actual point of impact was the dark hole at the center of Hal Brognola's left ear.

BROGNOLA PUT DOWN his knife and fork. Mixing the red wine and the chicken cacciatore had been a big mistake. The helping of garlic fococcia bread had compounded it. Even though he'd taken the precaution of loading his stomach with antacid before he started eating, the spicy combination was acting like battery acid in his stomach.

How could something that tasted so good, hurt so bad?

He removed a new bottle of antacid tablets from his suit jacket's side pocket, broke the outer antitamper seals with a thumbnail, then attacked the childproof cap. It opened, all right, but much more easily than he had expected. Fat white tablets cascaded onto his lap and then the floor.

"Damn," he muttered, automatically bending to pick them up. As he did, the plate-glass window shattered, chunks and splinters of glass sweeping across the table, raining on him. The air blast of the following round brushed against his scalp, and the glass in an antique mirror against the back wall cascaded to the floor.

Brognola turned the bend into a lazy shoulder roll out of the chair. For a moment he lay stunned amid the broken glass, then his highly trained brain kicked in—two shots, one shot to break the glass, the second to kill. From under the table he could see the three-story building directly across the wide street. A two-man team, at least, positioned on the upper-floor windows or the roof. Professionals, probably military trained.

Around him the other restaurant patrons sat frozen with forks and knives in hand. A woman at the next table started to scream. It broke the tableau. Chairs scraped back, tables crashed over.

He told himself he had to move, too.

As he rolled away from the emptied window frame, a bullet struck him. Everything went black. His momentum was just enough to carry his body out of the line of fire. He ended up on his back, eyes shut. Hal Brognola lay very still as a pool of blood spread from beneath his head.

4

Carrying a cardboard tray laden with cafeteria doughnuts and paper cups of hot coffee, the Military Police security guard moved quickly down the hallway of Walter Reed Army Hospital. The elevator doors opened at the far end of the corridor, and two men in lab coats exited the double-wide car, pushing a sheet-shrouded gurney ahead of them.

As the MP and the orderlies passed each other, under the glare of the overhead fluorescent lights the guard caught the black glint of a body bag through the gurney's sheet. It didn't surprise him. They always covered the cold ones when they had to move them through the corridors. They didn't want to scare the live patients. From a distance of ten feet, the orderlies' plastic-laminated credential tags looked perfectly valid.

If the MP had taken more than a passing glance, he would have seen that their shoes were all wrong. They weren't hospital shoes or even joggers, but black ballistic nylon, the kind of footwear that SWAT teams wore. If he had stopped them, he would have certainly noticed the unusual bulges under their loose-fitting coats, bulges that would have proved to be lanyard-slung, silenced 9 mm Beretta 93-Rs and clusters of stun grenades clipped to combat harnesses. If the guard had stared into the ice blue eyes of the taller of the two, he would have thought about reaching for his weapon.

But the MP did nothing. He continued on into the elevator and down to his patrol car, where sat a partner in serious need of junk food.

And that saved him from a world of pointless hurt.

The men in lab coats rolled the gurney and the body bag that contained Hal Brognola to the helicopter pad. As they approached the black Sikorsky helicopter with Justice Department markings, its turbines started their preflight whine. Three other men, these in tactical blacksuits, body armor and communications headsets, stood alongside the helicopter, with drawn Heckler & Koch MP-5 K machine pistols. They helped the lab-coated men load the gurney and its contents into the helicopter's main cabin and strap it down.

When they were airborne, wheeling over the lights of D.C., the pilot's voice crackled through the headsets. One of the men in black passed the word through his cupped hand to the taller of the "orderlies," who wasn't wired for sound. "Mack, Grimaldi says it's time to wake the dead."

The first thing Hal Brognola saw as the bag was unzipped was the face of Mack Bolan.

"Welcome back to the world of the living," the Executioner said over the rotor noise.

The big Fed gratefully sucked in fresh air. Head to foot, he was bathed in sweat. He levered himself up on an elbow. Belted into the jump seats along the wall were David McCarter, Gary Manning and Rafael Encizo, veteran warriors of Phoenix Force. They all gave him the thumbs-up sign.

Dressed in a medical coat, T. J. Hawkins, the newest member of the Phoenix Force covert-action team, started to help Bolan get Brognola out of the bag.

"No, I can do it," the Justice man insisted.

As it turned out, he couldn't do it.

He was as weak and trembly as a newborn kitten. The doctors had told him to expect that. The 7.62 mm hollowpoint round had cut a neat, shallow groove across the back of his head. An MRI scan had shown some minor brain swelling caused by the impact shock. The rear of his head sported a thick wad of bandage, and the hair around the wound was shaved to white scalp, which disinfectant had turned bright orange. Brognola's face and hands had numerous cut marks on them; there were still some needles of glass in his fingers. He had adamantly refused all pain medication, except aspirin, insisting that his head had to stay clear.

Bolan and Hawkins guided him off the gurney and into a waiting wheelchair, which was also strapped to the deck. The effort of movement brought Brognola some extra pain, which was clearly etched in the lines at the corners of his eyes. The back of his skull felt like it had been hit by a truck, and the massive dose of aspirin he had taken hadn't even scratched his world-class headache.

As far as the Washington press corps knew, the Justice Department's White House liaison was still at Walter Reed, in critical condition in a secure, locked-down area of the hospital. He wasn't expected to live. According to the plan approved by the President, that's where and how official press releases would keep him until the situation was resolved.

Grimaldi set down the Sikorsky on a grass general-aviation strip twenty miles outside D.C. There, to confuse any pursuit, McCarter, Manning and Encizo departed from the group in a rented Ford van. Bolan, Hawkins and Grimaldi moved Brognola to another helicopter, this one unmarked. Then they flew low and fast toward Virginia's Blue Ridge Mountains and the high-tech fortress of Stony Man Farm.

STONY MAN'S electronic-intel crew couldn't hide its concern as Hal Brognola, his face pale and drawn, slowly wheeled himself into the computer lab. From their respective workstations, Carmen Delahunt, Dr. Huntington Wethers and Akira Tokaido radiated genuine sympathy and anger, as did Barbara Price, the mission controller. Price was standing on the elevated dais beside the Farm's resident cybernetics specialist, Aaron "the Bear" Kurtzman. Behind his huge, horseshoe-shaped desk, Kurtzman was also wheelchair bound. The big, blocky man had permanently lost the use of his legs during an attack on Stony Man Farm.

It was Kurtzman who spoke first. "How are you doing, Hal? You look like hell."

"I can't stand up, but I can think," Brognola said, ascending the shallow ramp to the dais with the help of Mack Bolan, who stepped up to push the chair from behind.

"I know the feeling," Kurtzman said, giving him a grin.

"Where do you want to start on this, Hal?" Price asked. "You've heard about Ed Hartwell and his wife? Apparently the bastards killed her just to draw him out."

"I briefed him on the flight in," Bolan told her.

"I think it's safe to assume that the attacks were work-related," Brognola said. "Let's run a cross-check on Hartwell, Patachi and me. We need to catalog the operations some or all of us had in common."

"Already done," Tokaido announced. "There's only one operation that you all were part of—it's code-named R."

"Yeah, that's the way I remember it," Brognola said.

"I hacked into the file," Tokaido went on, "but it's been sanitized. According to the access log, six months ago it was reduced from almost a meg of data to a measly 4*K*. All it contains now is a shortlist of eight names, drawn from various government agencies."

"We know at least two of the people on the list are dead," Brognola said.

Kurtzman pivoted to address Hunt Wethers. "Check the other names on the list, Hunt, and see if they're alive."

"I'm on it." The ex-Berkeley cybernetics professor began to access the Farm's web of on-line data banks.

"Are you going to tell us what R is?" Price asked.

"Was," Brognola corrected her. "What R *was.*"

"All the more reason we should know about it," she said. Her interest was both personal and professional. To do her job, she needed to know what she was sending her people up against and why.

Brognola didn't answer her immediately. "Can I get something to drink?" he asked. "My mouth is really dry. The doctors said I'd be dehydrated from the blood loss."

"Orange juice?" she asked.

"Fine."

The woman fetched a bottle from the never empty ice chest behind her.

"I'm not trying to be cute, here, Barbara," he told her as he accepted the plastic bottle. "I just want to have all the facts in front of me before I start briefing you."

The reports came back quickly. Wethers read them off the screen. "Your Colombian DAS man, Augustin Murillo, was found in a dump outside Bogotá six days ago. His throat had been cut, his tongue pulled out the slit and his genitals had been severed and placed in his mouth. The El Salvadoran lieutenant-colonel died in a suspicious helicopter crash in Morazán province two days ago. Apparently his body was charred beyond recognition."

"The facts are in, Hal," Price said. "Four out of eight are dead."

Brognola didn't resent her insistence or her impatient tone. She was just doing her job.

"R was an action-oversight group tasked with bringing down the Medellín cartel," he said. "None of you knew about it because it was organized, funded and operational outside the Stony Man loop. R pulled international strings, made matériel arrangements, private agreements, transferred hard currency and lines of credit. Part of the program included the hiring and transport of two foreign sniper teams that were to assassinate and otherwise harass the cartel inside Colombia, this with DAS's full knowledge and consent.''

Brognola looked up at Bolan. The big guy gave him the slightest of nods.

They were on the same page.

''And did they?'' Kurtzman said.

''No. The snipers never did anything, as far as we could tell. We lost contact with both units right after they entered the country. Apparently they made no hits on the Medellín cartel. They certainly never asked for any blood money. We assumed that they were killed by cartel hit men.''

''You may want to revise that judgment now,'' the Executioner told him.

Kurtzman turned to his console, his fingers flying over the keyboard. As he typed, he talked. ''I'll access the DAS criminal-investigation files for Colombian assassinations similar to the Hartwell-Patachi hits. The search parameters will be based on weapon type and caliber, and the shooting distances involved. What was the snipers' date of insertion?''

Brognola told him. They waited in silence until the data scrolled up, then Kurtzman relayed it to them.

''There have been seventy-eight killings that fit the profile since February of 1993. None were strikes against the Medellín, however. They start with a series of murders of Cali-cartel higher-ups, then expand to political and judicial killings, government liberals, union organizers. From the notations I see sprinkled through here, the DAS analysts assumed the shooters were either British or Israeli mercs working for Medellín. They hypothesized that the killers were based out of the cartel's assassin-training camp in

Puerto Boyacá. This was never confirmed. No suspects were ever identified.''

''I think you've found your missing El Salvadoran shooters,'' Bolan said to Brognola.

''How do you know they're El Salvadoran?'' Price said.

Bolan glanced down at Hal as he spoke. ''We met, briefly, a few years ago.''

''As a personal favor to me, Striker did a quick field check on two military sniper teams in El Salvador. To be honest, at the time I was hoping the El Salvadorans would turn out to be incompetents. That was the only possible way I could've scuttled the lethal-harassment idea.'' Brognola's eyes flashed at the memory of his frustration. ''R was a majority-rules operation. I didn't have make-or-break authority on any of the specific missions we launched.''

''So they passed the field test,'' Kurtzman said. ''How good were they?''

''Better than average when I last saw them,'' Bolan said. ''For several years they've had an open hunting season. I think we can assume they've used it to polish up their act.''

''Who are these guys?'' Price demanded.

''El Salvadoran military records going back more than ten years showed nothing out of the ordinary or suspicious,'' Brognola said. ''There was no connection with known death-squad people or criminal activity. At the time I thought they were too good to be true, but I couldn't prove anything. And the other members of R didn't care if the snipers' backgrounds were bullshit. They wanted men who would do a dirty, dangerous job, and who couldn't be traced back to them.''

''Wait a minute,'' Bolan interjected. ''In El Salvador, on the return from the KZ in the van, these guys were talking about sex killings during a military operation. Sounded like all four of them participated, or maybe they just wanted me to think they had. At the time, I couldn't tell whether they were just trying to impress me. I don't recall much of the details."

"I can cross-check verified military involvement in rape and murder in El Salvador," Tokaido said, typing in the search parameters.

The answer came back in about forty seconds.

"Does the Atlacatl Battalion ring any bells?" he asked.

"Jesus," Brognola muttered.

"I have a major incident in Morazán province in December 1981," Tokaido went on. "It was part of Operación Rescate, a government attempt to rid the province of ERP rebels. Elements of the Atlacatl surrounded and captured the village of El Mozote. Even though the townspeople had never supported the guerrillas and they didn't resist the invasion, the soldiers robbed, then murdered more than nine hundred of them, including hundreds of small children. They dragged the older girls and young women up to La Cruz, a nearby mountain, where they staked them out and raped them for an entire day before shooting them to death or chopping their heads off with machetes."

"The snipers mentioned something about La Cruz," Bolan said. "Yeah, I remember, now. *La cruz* means 'the cross.' 'Virgins on the Cross,' is what they said. It stuck in my head at the time because I remember thinking it was some kind of a fouled-up religious reference. And the town name, El Mozote, that sounds familiar to me, too."

"Who recommended these guys?" Carmen Delahunt asked.

"The dead lieutenant-colonel," Brognola said. "He also provided their documentation. He was R's only link to the snipers, and we were assured by him that the link was indirect, with several cutouts between them and him."

"Run all his known names—together, separately and in all combinations—against a list of the Atlacatl ranks," Bolan suggested.

After a couple of minutes of computer search, Tokaido had the answer. "I have a Captain Francisco S. Gomez. He's the right age for our dead guy."

"Can we get some photo ID on the five of them?" Price said.

Meanwhile, Kurtzman had already pulled up the State-CIA-Justice intel on the Atlacatl Battalion. "I would call these guys 'animals,' but that would give animals a bad name. One of their male-bonding rituals is to slit the bellies of the farmyard cows and pigs they've shot and take turns drinking the warm blood and smearing it over their faces. It's part of their machismo-to-the-max hype. Supposed to terrify the guerrillas, but of course the livestock belongs to the unarmed peasants.

"The Atlacatl are nothing but a gang of murderers and looters hiding behind army uniforms, operating with auto-weapons and artillery cover. In and out of the field, they stick together and support one another. In return they collect payoffs and kickbacks. Since the peace accords were signed, several attempts have been made to break them up, but nothing has worked."

"I don't think these Central American child rapers could have orchestrated our killings in D.C.," Price said. "We're talking distance and logistics here, and that means finance and manpower. They might have known what and who R was, but even so, they don't have any apparent motive, aside from money, for hunting down the members."

"The Medellín cartel does have a motive, though," Brognola said. "The crackdown that was stage-managed by R put an end to them. Our Colombian amigos are big on revenge. They like it hot or cold. It would be right up their alley to use sniper teams made up of foreign nationals."

"Who's left on the Medellín most-wanted list?" Bolan said.

"How far down do you want me to go?" Kurtzman asked.

"It has to be someone with clout," Price said. "That means money and infrastructure."

"Start at the top," Bolan said.

"That would be one Raffi del Borgo, a.k.a. el Sicarito. The nickname refers to his apprenticeship during the Emerald Wars. From 1971 to 1979, freewheeling gangsters, many of Lebanese or Syrian extraction, fought over the country's gem mines. Their private armies of assassins kept the mine workers in line, eliminated the competition and settled scores. Del Borgo was the youngest of the Emerald Wars' contract killers. He logged close to one hundred kills before he was twenty. That's how he made his bones in the early days. Like many other of the emerald entrepreneurs, he moved into coca in early 1980s when the Medellín cartel was formed. Prior to the crackdown he was an underlord. Now he's a king without a kingdom. DAS believes he's no longer in Colombia. I'm printing his mug shot now."

"Poor guy, all he has is truckloads of dirty money," Delahunt said.

"Maybe not," Brognola countered. "We did a pretty righteous job of asset seizure on those Medellín boys. Shut them off from their capital in Colombia, but good. If this guy left home, he might have gotten out with nothing but the designer shirt on his back."

"And a great big grudge," Kurtzman commented.

"Wouldn't he want to personally supervise his revenge?" Tokaido said.

"Do you think he's currently in the U.S.?" Price asked Brognola.

"It's very possible."

"Then let's track his holdings here," Tokaido suggested. "Maybe we can use them to find out where he's gone to ground."

"Justice hasn't been able to do much with the money trail," Brognola admitted, "but then again, they're not looking to just corner the guy so they can terminate him. They're interested in forfeiture and confiscation of drug assets, and that takes hard evidence that will stand up in court."

"I think I've got a possible search path for us," Kurtzman said. "We can pick up where Justice left off, using its data base. We may be able to connect his friends and family to large land or business purchases in the States, which will give us possible current locations for Señor del Borgo. If that doesn't work, we'll move on to their friends and family."

"If he's being forced to convert his holdings back to cash now," Wethers said, "that could help narrow our search."

"It could, but no matter how you cut it, this is going to take a while to nail down," Kurtzman warned.

"In the meantime," Brognola said, "there are still four people on the R list who are out in the cold."

"I can do something about that," Price told him.

"Something else you've got to consider, Hal," Bolan said as the mission controller stepped quickly to a secure phone.

"What's that?"

"Somebody on the list gave all of you up to the cartel."

"Yeah, that occurred to me."

Price returned shortly. "We've got containment. CIA is going to handle security for its own people. Justice is pulling in the other two. In a couple of hours everyone should be out of danger."

5

"We have a slight problem," Ted Reese said, putting down the phone. As he straightened, he adjusted the hang of the stainless-steel Smith & Wesson .357 Magnum pistol under his left armpit. "The Army tactical unit has been delayed en route. A semi truck accident on the Beltway has got the whole thing blocked off."

"Super," Dick Albright said, shaking his head.

Bob Sutro visibly sagged at the news. "What about the chopper? Do we still have transportation?"

"The helicopter is waiting in a field along the parkway," Reese told him. "As soon as we can get you safely convoyed over there, you'll go directly to either Fort Belvoir or Andrews."

Albright glanced around the comfortable Alexandria, Virginia, condominium. It was Agency property, a safehouse. He and Sutro had been picked up at their respective D.C. homes by the agency security team at around 9:00 p.m. and driven directly to the two-story building. They had been stuck there all night, sitting as far away from the windows as they could get.

For a while, it had looked as if they were going to have to stay there for the duration. It took some convincing to make their higher-ups believe the threat level warranted their isolation at a secure military base. Initially their superiors were only looking at the three attacks so far, which appeared to be individual or small-unit actions. They believed the six armed inside men assigned to the safehouse were adequate protection; there were no countersnipers assigned to the rooftops of the condo complex. They were relying on the assumptions that Sutro and Albright were well concealed, and that no one had followed them.

Somebody somewhere along the chain of command got some fresh information and changed the decision. Instead of reinforcing their current position with additional men and potentially jeopardizing its secrecy, Sutro and Albright were going to be moved to a site with an existing perimeter defense. That decision had been made three hours earlier. Since then, they had been nervously waiting for the cavalry to escort them to safety.

"Think of it this way," Paul Mills said, looking up from the paperback he was reading. On the dining-room table in front of him was a silenced MAC-10 machine pistol and several spare 30-round magazines. "You're getting the chance to look at lethal harassment from a whole new angle."

"Yeah," added Mark Nevins, who stood by the narrow window that flanked the condo's front door. Rosy light was starting to filter through the floor-to-ceiling draperies. "There's another monograph in here somewhere, guys."

Very funny, Albright thought sourly. He was glad that the other security guys were upstairs and had missed the joke. Of course, it was bound to get around, anyway. There were a lot of jealous people who would enjoy it back at Langley, people who envied the way they had staked out their claim and how successfully they had defended it against all comers.

Sutro didn't look good at all. As he sipped at what had to be his tenth cup of coffee, his face had a blank, inward-staring expression. Sutro was the "idea man" of the pair. He brainstormed, and Albright followed after him with a shovel and broom. Though their psy-ops collaborations had been successful, the work had been particularly hard on Albright. Usually the stuff Sutro gave him was so ill thought out that you could hardly call it more than blithering. Their interactive process required him to ask Sutro what he meant. Over and over. Often Sutro himself didn't know what he meant until he was closely questioned by his partner. It wasn't command-of-language problems. Sutro could write well enough. It was more of a let-Dick-do-it thing.

They had some serious work to do as soon as they were safe at Andrews Air Force Base or Fort Belvoir. They had to prepare the spin-doctoring on the El Salvadoran snipers, in case the blinds came up on the whole thing. The international-incident consequences aside, their theories about the utility of lethal harassment certainly hadn't been validated by the events in Colombia. However, as long as they were prepared to stand in there, they could survive it. Maybe they would take a short-term hit, get stuck with some punk assignments, but in a year or less, they would be back on top, everything would have been forgiven and forgotten. Even the damage to the credibility of their bailiwick, psy ops, would have been repaired. That was the way the bureaucratic system worked—hang in, hang on, make retirement.

"You see anything out there?" Reese asked Mills.

He stepped to a front picture window and edged back the corner of the drape. "No. Nothing's moving. Nobody's up, yet. I guess they're all sleeping in on Sunday."

They all heard the sound of a vehicle pulling into the parking area.

Bob Sutro went rigid in his chair. A chill ran up Albright's spine and he took an automatic half step back toward the kitchen.

"Will you guys lighten up?" Mills said. "It's just a newspaper-delivery guy in a scuzzy station wagon. Orange bill cap, black T-shirt, jeans, white joggers. Man, he looks like he had a Saturday night to remember."

"Watch him," Reese said. He keyed his belt transmitter, then spoke to the men in the upstairs bedrooms. "Got a newspaper guy moving around outside."

"See him," came the response through the walkie-talkie's speaker.

"Anything else?"

"All clear from up here."

Reese clapped a hand on Sutro's shoulder. The slightly overweight black man winced. "Hey, relax. You've got nothing to worry about. The situation's under control. If we need civilian backup, it can be here inside of five minutes. Short of an air assault, you're going to be just fine."

ALPHONSO WATCHED the curtain drop back in place behind the condo's window. He could have taken the shot, glass or no glass. Aiming for center torso, even if the bullet had deflected, he would have hit the guy somewhere. But that wasn't the plan. Everything was arranged, timed.

The newspaper deliveryman went from door to door along the line of condos, dropping a rolled paper beside their front doors. It took him a second longer in front of the safehouse door. Instead of dropping the paper on the welcome mat, he hung it on the doorknob. Alphonso immediately pushed the chronograph button on his LED watch. Preset for two minutes, it began counting down.

Along with the morning news, the CIA was getting a healthy dose of plastic explosive.

The deliveryman got back in his station wagon and drove out of the parking area. He was a Colombian, one of the dozen in proximity to the safehouse. Most of them were hidden behind the redbrick, Georgian condo block Alphonso and Rigo were shooting from. The snipers were in position in a second-story window across the parking lot and directly opposite from the CIA condo.

Behind Alphonso and Rigo, a young man lay dead in a pool of darkening blood on the mattress of a queen-size bed. Naked but for his briefs, the midlevel government bureaucrat was the owner-occupant of the condo. He had awakened as two intruders burst into his bedroom, but he had never made it out of his bed. Rigo had held a pillow over the man's face while Alphonso set the point of a nine-inch bowie knife against his chest and, driving with his full weight, stabbed it in to the hilt. It had taken him three such savage thrusts to locate and pierce the man's heart. The El Salvadorans had dragged the mattress bearing the corpse off the box springs and into a corner of the bedroom.

Thirty seconds showed on the LED.

Rigo sprayed the aluminum window track with a miniature can of lubricant and slid the window open. Then he returned to their makeshift shooting platform and got behind the scoped and sandbagged M-1 A.

They had dragged the bed frame and box springs in front of the window. On them they had stacked sets of box springs and mattresses taken from the other bedroom. They had created a four-foot-high, prone shooting platform by putting a couple of the condo's interior doors side by side on top of the pile. From this elevated position they both had clear fire lanes to the front door and windows of the CIA condo. The distance to target was under fifty yards.

Alphonso's wristwatch beeped. Outside, the Colombians swarmed around the sides of their condo block.

The snipers' breathing slowed. They were after targets of opportunity. Alphonso had the downstairs, Rigo the upstairs.

The plastique detonated with a flash, blowing the condo's front door inward. The Colombians slid behind the parked cars, within ten yards of the safehouse entryway.

Alphonso picked up a target as it staggered through the smoke, across the gap between the splintered doorjambs. The match-grade trigger broke cleanly under his fingertip's pressure, and the gun bucked hard against his shoulder.

THE CONCUSSION of the explosion slammed Albright back against the stair rail. The door crashed to the floor and acrid smoke billowed into the room. Nevins, who had been standing beside the door, stepped out. Albright could see blood pouring from the man's ears, his face smoke blackened, his eyes shut. Everything was happening in a sickening blur.

Then Nevins's face exploded, a cavern opening up where his right eye had been, and he was driven forward, sprawling onto the fallen door.

Reese forgot about the wheelgun under his arm and lunged for the suppressed MAC-10 on the dining-room table. Sutro broke from his armchair, running Albright's way, head down, arms pumping.

As Sutro bolted past him, heading for the kitchen and the condo's back door, Albright saw shadows moving behind the smoke hanging in the doorway. He had waited a split second too long. It was too late for him to make the rear exit. They would shoot him in the back before he made the kitchen archway. Having no other option, he streaked up the stairs. From behind him came the muffled sounds of silenced machine pistols exchanging fire at close range.

As Albright sprinted down the hallway, heavy slugs tore through the windows and walls of the front bedroom, punching ragged divots in the wallpapered plasterboard to his left. The prone, unmoving body of one of his bodyguards lay sprawled across the corridor. He hurdled it.

"Don't shoot! It's me!" he cried, diving through the door of the back bedroom.

The two surviving security men looked ashen. One of

them moved to position by the door, gamely covering the hallway with his autopistol. The other guy punched 911 into his cellular phone.

Before his call was picked up by the dispatcher, the upper floor of the condo was rocked by another explosion. The concussion grenade put the man at the door flat on his butt. Heavy feet thundered down the hallway, and 9 mm parabellum slugs gnawed at the door frame.

"Bail! We've got to bail!" The security guy dropped the phone and threw back the window.

Albright didn't hesitate. He scrambled out the window onto the sloping roof. As he did so, the wall behind him shuddered from dozens of bullet impacts. The high-velocity slugs blasted off fist-sized chunks of the quarter-inch-thick decorative brick facing on the outside wall. Inside the bedroom, the security men were being ground into hamburger.

The back of the CIA condo opened onto another parking lot, and across the stretch of asphalt stood another identical block of redbrick buildings. If Albright could make it that far, he thought he had a fighting chance. But first it was a fifteen-foot drop from the edge of the steep roof to the ground. No time to be graceful. He was sliding on his butt down the shingles when his right shoulder blew apart. He couldn't do as he planned and grab the gutter on the way down to break his fall. He slid off the roof like a skier off a chute, landing almost squarely on the limp body of Bob Sutro.

FROM HIS POSITION in the second story of a vacant condo across the parking area, Gaspar saw the black CIA man preparing to duck away from the condo's back door. He guessed the man would be moving to the left, as that direction led to the closest solid cover, a big tree. Gaspar used the trap technique, swinging the cross hairs away from the door, holding at the proper lead distance for a running man. When the target pushed the door open and Gaspar saw the first blur of movement, he fired.

The hollowpoint bullet chopped the CIA man down in midstride and sent him crashing hard to the ground. He didn't move after that. Gaspar put the Duplex aim point on his head and shot him again, just to make sure.

A split second after Gaspar fired, Tacho's weapon roared.

Gaspar saw the white man on the condo roof clutch at his shoulder, then continue sliding. "Not dead!" he said, marking the shot.

"*¡Mierda!*" Tacho swore as the man plummeted from the roof. Through the Leupold scope, he followed his target down. The CIA man landed on his backside, legs draped over the black guy's carcass. He just sat there, stunned.

Tacho fired again.

The seated man's head snapped back as the 168-grain boattail slammed it, then slowly, almost lazily, he toppled onto his side.

Gaspar checked his watch as they vacated the hide. Three minutes had elapsed from start to finish. A car waited for them in the parking area. Before the first neighbor even started to think about calling the police, all of the hired guns were moving swiftly out of the KZ.

6

Ocala, Florida

With the shower's needle spray peppering the skin of her back, Brenda Lee Baker attacked her front side with a loofah sponge, doing her best to scour off reminders of her all-night encounter with the ranch's new guest—a military type from Central America. Like most Latins, he couldn't seem to get enough of her. It was the natural-blond thing, she told herself as she worked up a rich lather. It drove them crazy.

"Oh, hell!" she snarled. High up on the inside of her thighs, overlaid sets of bite marks were already circled with ugly, purpling bruises.

Baker got her paycheck whether she did anybody or not. She was live-in help at the lavish Florida horse farm. She got a generous five-figure monthly stipend, and free board and room in the cabana house. She had worked up an impressive stock portfolio in the past three years. Two more at this wage scale, and she could leave the life behind forever.

In some cases, she didn't mind the work at all; in others, like the guy last night, if she'd had a choice, she would have given it a wide miss. As part of her job, she had slept with visiting killers before, mostly South Americans. Some of them had been surprisingly gentle, but not this one. There was something unclean about him. It wasn't just that under his expensive cologne, there was a sour, bacterial odor to him. And he put out threat vibes that wouldn't quit. The look in his eyes during their most intimate moments said that he'd like nothing better than to cut her head off and keep it in the freezer as a love toy.

"Hey, baby," said a voice on the other side of the shower-stall door, "you ready for more?"

Hell, no, Baker thought, shutting off the water.

The frosted-glass pane slid back. Naked, still beaded with sex sweat, Suarez approached her, leering.

"I don't think so," she said, glancing down. "You're not up to it."

She knew from the way his eyes flashed that the words were a big mistake.

"Think again," he said, lunging into the shower.

There was nowhere for her to retreat. He seized her by the neck and pinned her back to the shower wall, driving his forearm against the front of her throat. He strangled her like that for a good half minute, and she thought for sure he was going to kill her then and there. When the edges of her consciousness started to go fuzzy, she stopped struggling.

"Suarez!"

The voice from the other room froze the El Salvadoran.

"Suarez, get in here!"

"Of course, Señor del Borgo, right away," the colonel said. As he released her, he gave her a contemptuous look and said, "I can take you anytime I want. Remember that." He moved away from her and grabbed a robe from a hook behind the bathroom door.

Because he turned away from the shower immediately, he missed the expression on Baker's face. Not that he would have understood the depth of feeling behind it, anyway. Suarez wasn't used to seeing that particular brand of fury on the faces of the women he abused. To him, women were objects. And real macho men didn't fear warm, well-upholstered pieces of furniture.

"I'M GOING TO NEED another whore very soon," Suarez said as he plopped himself down on a white leather couch across from the Colombian drug lord. He gestured toward the bathroom with a thumb. "I'm going to wear that one out in a day or so. I'm kind of rough on whores."

"No problem," Raffi del Borgo said.

"I'd appreciate another blonde."

Baker exited the bathroom, clad in a towel. She dressed quickly in front of them, pulling on beige stirrup pants and a turtleneck, and knee-high brown leather boots. "I'm going out for a ride," she announced to del Borgo as she walked out the cabana door. She didn't even look at Suarez.

"She is in love with me," Suarez confided to the man seated across from him. "She knows how dangerous it is, but you know what they say about the moth and the flame."

Del Borgo took hold of the massive gold, emerald and diamond ring on his middle finger and twisted it around and around.

Suarez noticed the gesture.

It wasn't, as he thought, a movement brought on by nervousness.

The drug lord continued to rotate the huge emerald. He could have warned his house guest about Brenda, but he chose not to do so. Like most of the high-ranking El Salvadorans that he had dealt with, this officer was a stupid, arrogant man. Del Borgo blamed this squarely on the softness of his upbringing. He had come from a solidly middle-class family, with advantages of education, position and old-boy network that del Borgo as a rural peasant child had only dreamed of. Suarez had succeeded without effort, without talent, based on an accident of birth. Because he had no skills and no real accomplishments, Suarez could only feast on his own bloated vision of himself, and because he enjoyed the taste so much, he allowed it, in turn, to distort reality.

All he saw was the ring and the gesture.

That the faceted green stone might have any significance beyond the superficial, extravagant display of wealth would never have occurred to the colonel. If he had possessed even the smallest curiosity, an interest in anything outside himself, he would have asked.

And if he had asked, he wouldn't have smiled when he saw the ring touched so.

The garish thing was a tangible representation of hundreds of human souls, victims released to their Maker through del Borgo's effort, and many by the strength of his own two hands. The ring had been a present to himself, a reminder of the mountain he had climbed, from hired assassin to emerald king. The central stone had come from one of his own mines, mines that he had acquired and controlled with more murder. His move to coca had been a natural one: del Borgo had perfected all the necessary business tools.

"I was told you were making some loud threats last night about what you might do if you aren't paid," del Borgo said. "Threats are not a good idea."

"All I want is my money. When will it be here?"

The drug lord was tired of hearing about Suarez's money. He shrugged. "The Miami real-estate deal closes tomorrow. When that's done, you'll get it."

To del Borgo the price he had already paid seemed too high. The faked death in the helicopter, the false ID and the transport out of El Salvador had added up to ten or fifteen thousand dollars U.S. In El Salvador he could have had the man killed four times for a tenth of that amount.

As he looked at Suarez, he considered whether he really needed him around until tomorrow.

"I'll expect all my money, then." The colonel rose. "If we have nothing further to discuss, I'm going to take a shower."

Del Borgo wasn't surprised that the man showed no interest in the fate of the snipers or the outcome of their mission. The drug lord, on the other hand, was concerned that the snipers wouldn't continue doing their jobs if they found out he had eliminated their former commanding officer. Not because they had any love for Suarez. If he turned up dead, they would think they were next. Which would have been a mistake, since del Borgo had no intention of throwing away such valuable men. Of hardy peasant stock, they had proved themselves to him many times in Colombia. Some of their hits were works of art.

And El Sicarito was a great connoisseur of hits.

In Urubá, they had killed a pro-trade unionist banana worker at seven hundred yards, shot him through the heart as he urinated against a wall. He lay dead, flat on his back in the road, taken out of this world by an invisible hand, like lightning from the fingertip of God. The Salvadorans had done much to spread fear of the cartel.

The other thing he liked about these snipers was their politics. They were as rabidly anti-Communist as he was. Which meant they made no distinction between an M-19 guerrilla and a union organizer, between a schoolteacher with liberal views and his wife and kids. The Medellín cartel had a history of backing right-wing vigilantes and death squads. Their hatred for the political left began in the late 1970s when drug lords were kidnapped by guerrillas and held for ransom.

Like his fellows in the Medellín cartel, del Borgo had spent much time, effort and money buying into the social structure of Colombia—their influence ran through it like threads of cancer. In its heyday the coca industry had employed half a million people, which was equal to all other manufacturers combined. Del Borgo had bought cattle ranches and invested heavily in urban real estate. Then, hedging his bets, he had moved some of his working capital abroad.

A lucky decision, as it turned out.

The cartel had won control of their country, only to have the victory stolen from them by the illegal acts of an interfering superpower.

The vengeance he was taking wasn't for the other cartel members—Gacha, Ochoa, Escobar—who had been killed in the War on Drugs, but for himself, for his own loss. Thanks to R, his cash accounts in Colombia had been frozen, his real property seized. Hiring so many soldiers from the former Medellín-U.S. organization was an expensive proposition, requiring the sale of much of his Florida real estate. It was, however, worth every penny.

Only two members of the oversight group known as R were still alive.

And their time left in this world could be counted in tens of minutes.

7

From the bow of the fourteen-foot Zodiac inflatable raft, through the maze of overhanging branches, William "Wild Bill" Ransom of the FBI's Special Weapons Unit could see across the mirror-smooth surface of Virginia's Lake Margaret, which reflected brilliant blue sky and fleecy clouds, to the Fox Island Federal Wildlife Reservation. Fox Island was two acres of rock and scattered pines at the most remote end of the forty-mile-long lake, a third of a mile from the northwest shore. With binoculars Ransom surveyed the island's only house, a two-story gray field-stone-and-timber building that originally had been a coal magnate's hunting-and-fishing lodge. Armed Justice Department sentries moved back and forth on a broad porch that ran halfway around the perimeter of the building. All the wooden shutters on the windows were battened down.

"Echo, this is Rambler at Bravo Station," he said softly into the mike of his communication headset. "Request status check. Over."

"Roger, Rambler. Everything is okay. Nothing to report. Over."

Ransom thanked the communications man and signed off. Behind him in the Zodiac boat were five other men from Justice. They were dressed as he was, in black, with matching bill caps and body armor, all emblazoned with FBI. They carried shoulder-slung 9 mm German-made machine pistols and high-capacity semiauto pistols in shoulder leather. Behind the sixty-horsepower engine on the inflatable's wooden stern, lined up in the narrow cove like beads on a string, were three more identical boats and crews, with identical armament.

Even with the shade of the overhanging tree limbs, it was oppressively hot in the cove. They had been in position since early that morning, waiting for the bad guys to make their move on Fox Island.

And it was almost a sure bet that they would.

A search of the victims of the hit on the CIA safehouse had turned up an electronic bug in a shoe heel, which explained how the site had been located and targeted by the opposition. When a similar device had been discovered in the shoe of the DEA man, Freeberg, the powers that be had decided to use the bug to lure the killers into a trap at an isolated location.

Ransom scanned the island's rocky beach again. One man guarded the empty dock that jutted out into the bay behind the house. In addition to body armor, he wore a flat black Kevlar armored helmet. The man on the dock wasn't relying solely on his trauma plate, though: he kept on the move, and he moved erratically, not wanting to give the snipers an easy shot. An unguarded Justice Department helicopter sat on its skids on the stretch of green lawn in front of the house. There were enough armed men showing outside the house to make it look like it was defended—as it would have to be after the CIA hit earlier in the day—it just didn't look defended enough.

Which was the whole idea.

When the bad guys showed up and tried to take the island in a water assault, Ransom and company would come blazing out of their hiding place like demons from hell, and the gangsters would be caught between small-arms fire from the island and fire from the Zodiac boats.

Nowhere to run, nowhere to hide.

And SWU's standing orders were to kill anyone who resisted, which was just fine with the unit leader.

Hal Brognola had made a lot of friends in the department over the years, and one of them was Wild Bill Ransom.

DAN FREEBERG SWEPT the fingers and palm of his hand over the freckled, hairless dome of his head. He was in a tight spot. There was thirty bucks in the pot, the dealer had two eights showing and all he was holding was a pair of deuces.

"Come on, DEA," Eleanor McCullen said, tapping her fingernails on the deck in her hand. "Either you're in or you're out."

Alex Tidman, the FBI agent in charge of the Fox Island operation, took another sip of diet soda from the can in front of him, then said, "Hey, McCullen, don't push him. This is the biggest decision he's had to make all year."

"Give me two cards," Freeberg said.

The woman from State flicked them at him across the dining-room table.

As he turned up the corners of the cards, Freeberg's face drooped.

"A goner," Tidman pronounced.

"DOA," McCullen agreed, flipping her cards over to expose a third eight, then reaching for the pot.

Freeberg folded his arms over his chest. He shook his head. "You guys are too tough, I'm out of here."

"Stay, DEA," McCullen told him as she reshuffled. "Stay and learn something about the game of poker."

"You're cleaning me out," he protested.

"When you're broke, we'll switch to strip poker," Tidman said.

"Send him home in his skivvies?" McCullen said. "Now, there's a really scary thought."

"All right, all right, deal me in."

Tidman took an incoming message on his headset. He turned away from the others and spoke tersely into the minimike. "The word has just come down," he said as he turned back. "We're going to get a visit from some 'specialist' who's already en route. Otherwise, no problems. The mainland beach patrol just checked in. They haven't seen anything yet. The countersniper teams on the high ground report all clear, too. Maybe our friends are going to wait until after dark. Not that it will change the outcome."

Freeberg looked at the woman from State as she began to deal out fresh cards. Both of them were confident in Justice's plan or they would never have agreed to being the peanut butter in a rat trap. If the scumbags hadn't killed Ed and Kate Hartwell, orphaning their kids, Freeberg probably wouldn't have volunteered for the job. After all, he had a family to think about, too. But he wanted to see the men responsible for the murders dead and buried. And he was willing to put his own life on the line to make it so. He knew that's how McCullen felt, too.

Of course, as far as R was concerned, Freeberg knew it was shit-in-the-fan time. In some upper-echelon circles its existence had already been exposed; the details of its mission would soon come to light, as well. He wasn't overly concerned, however. It wouldn't be the first time an American President had trod heavily upon the sovereignty of the U.S.'s southern neighbors, and it wouldn't be the last, either. In this case, at any rate, there had been some positive results to the violation of national boundaries and treaties: a major blow to the Medellín cartel. That part would play extremely well in the press.

The DEA man took a moment to look around the room. He liked this place. It reminded him of a fishing lodge in Minnesota his father had taken him to one summer. Big old stone fireplace, timbered rafters in a high ceiling, couches with frames made of rough-hewn wood. The only concession they had made to the situation was to keep the heavy winter shutters closed, which meant they lost the beautiful view of the lake and the two low mountains on the other side. That's where the countersniper teams were.

TACHO AND HIS BROTHER, Gaspar, had little trouble locating their Justice Department opposite numbers on the wooded Virginia mountainside. From a tactical standpoint, there were really only two options open to the Feds: either occupy and hold the best hide on the hill, the one that controlled the seven-hundred-yard fire lanes to the island, or occupy a hide that allowed them to kill anyone trying to set up in the best shooting position. The two Justice countersnipers on the mountain assigned to the Ruiz brothers had chosen the latter.

The best hide was a large boulder outcrop near the summit that looked down on the island at about a forty-five-degree angle. The wall of rock had numerous deep clefts and platforms from which to shoot, and most of them were above or between the treetops.

Tacho and Gaspar had stalked into position on the mountainside well below the outcrop, moving a few inches at a time in their leaf-draped camo suits, pulling their long guns along in padded, similarly camouflaged drag-bags. Satisfied that the countersnipers were not hiding among the boulders, they began a careful search of the surrounding woods.

Through his minibinoculars, Gaspar spotted the shape of a booted foot one hundred feet up a pine tree. He looked through his rifle scope and saw the camo web straps that held the tree blind in place on the main trunk. Using hand signals, he informed his brother of the shooter's location and the fact that the countersnipers had split up to cover the primary hide with two intersecting angles of fire.

Answering in sign language, Tacho told Gaspar to move

into killing range of the first Fed, while he found and targeted the second. Since it would take him longer to do that, and the time needed was unknown, Tacho would take the first shot.

Again, because of the limitations of the terrain, finding the other FBI man wasn't difficult for the El Salvadoran. That Fed, too, had scaled a tree and set up a folding shooting seat high in its branches. The only problem Tacho had was finding a clear path for his shot amid all the tree limbs. There was none. So he had to take a dangerous course for a sniper: shortening the range to target.

Tacho crept his way to the base of the sniper's tree, then, putting the trunk between himself and the man in the perch, he unlimbered his camo-taped M-1 A. With the additional length of the SCRC suppressor, it felt a bit clumsy as he turned it in his hands. Above him about seventy-five feet, he could see the Fed's boot heels and legs and the camouflaged underside of the plywood seat. He slid down onto his back beside the tree trunk and pointed the rifle up through the lower limbs. Only when he was in firing position did he flip up the scope's lens covers, giving his target no time to react even if he caught the sun's flash off the Leupold's objective lens. Tacho put the Duplex cross hairs where he thought the man's tailbone would be and took up the trigger slack.

The SCRC suppressor tamed the .308's usual 168-decibel bellow, making it softer than the report of a .22. The destructive force of the bullet was unchanged, however. The plywood seat shattered and split, and the man sitting in it let out a shrill cry of surprise and pain. The federal countersniper had tied himself to the tree, as well. As the seat gave way under him, he was left suddenly dangling from the camo straps, legs jerking in the air.

Tacho rolled out of the way as a gush of blood rained

from the treetop. He stood and fired again, putting an end to the aerial jig dance.

GASPAR HEARD the cry and the muffled noise of two quick shots. It sounded like someone was potting a few squirrels out of season. He found the stock's spot weld with his cheek and lined up his own shot. Figuring that the man had to be wearing body armor, Gaspar aimed for the boot-laced seam that ran from armpit to waist.

The Fed sniper whispered into his headset, asking his partner to confirm that shots had been fired. The only answer he got was a boattail hollowpoint through the heart. His scoped rifle crashed through the branches and stuck, muzzle first, in the soft dirt at the base of the tree.

Gaspar met his brother at the foot of the boulder outcrop. They quickly climbed into position near the top of the bluff and set up their hide. When that was done, Tacho pressed his radio transmitter's tone key, producing a single, half-second note that informed the respective assault teams that they had total control of their sector of the high ground. Almost at once, the transmitter beeped back another tone signal, this one with two notes. Rigo and Alphonso had taken the other mountaintop.

With Gaspar acting as spotter, the Ruiz brothers began to take bearings on the house and grounds, figuring the compensation for their relatively steep downward shooting angle.

There were plenty of human targets for them to range on.

LES JOHNSON TOOK a grease pencil from his shirt pocket and drew a circle and X on the inside of the Cessna 180's windshield.

"X marks the spot, Buckwheat," he said to the stocky man in the headset sitting in the copilot's seat.

The Colombian passenger looked suddenly doubtful. "Are you sure this will work?"

"Sure, I'm sure. This is T-LAR targeting. I could do it in my sleep," the grizzled ex-military pilot said. "Hell, I've done it in my sleep."

Under each of the wings of the stolen float plane, at a measured distance from the fuselage's centerline, Johnson had bolted two hollow tubes. Each tube he then packed with a 2.75-inch, high-explosive antipersonnel rocket. The rockets' ignition wires ran from the backs of the tubes along the wings and into both sides of the cockpit through the windows. Johnson had hooked all the wires up to a single electrical switch, which he had taped securely to the dashboard.

"Like I told you, we used this same routine in Vietnam to mark targets for our fighter jets. First in the old O-1 Bird Dog, then in the Cessna O-2."

His passenger received this information with a blank expression.

"Hey, if I dick up this little job," Johnson continued, "I give you permission to blow my brains out."

More blank stare.

"Aw, just buckle up," Johnson growled, and started the engine.

After the Colombian had snapped his over-the-shoulder safety belt into the seat fitting, Johnson brought the Cessna 180 up to takeoff speed on the glass-smooth lake, then he eased back on the yoke. The float plane lifted off, maybe a bit sluggish in the controls, but no big deal. It pleased him that the extra weight and drag of the rockets and their homemade pods hadn't totally loused up the Cessna's aerodynamics. Not that the flight was going to be long enough to make that a factor, anyway.

Johnson climbed to twenty-five hundred feet before he

began to bank gently, coming around to the heading for the rocket assault.

A TRIO OF NINETEEN-FOOT Boston Whaler Outrage boats drifted along the shoreline four miles east of Fox Island, apparently rafted together while some of their occupants fished and others sunned themselves on the foredecks. Inspection by a boarding party would have shown things weren't as normal as they appeared. The "sunbathers" were, in fact, fully clothed. The "anglers" were fishing without line, hooks, sinkers or bait. The three boats weren't secured to one another by lines; they were being held together by the passengers. And the big 250-horsepower outboards bolted to the vessels' transoms were growling and mumbling at idle.

Two sets of tone signals sounded through a hand-held transmitter that lay on the dash of the middle boat's control console.

"*¡Vamos!*" the skipper of the center boat shouted.

The weekend-boat-party ruse went over the side, along with all the fishing rods. After shoving the hulls apart, the passengers picked up MAC-10s and Uzis from between their feet on the deck. They held on to the side rails as, rooster tails of spray flying, the center console boats roared up on plane. Even with ten men to a boat, they were doing fifty miles per hour in a heartbeat. In V-formation, they screamed along the lake's northern shoreline.

One of the Colombian boating enthusiasts let loose a shout and waved his hand in the air, pointing behind them. The others turned to look.

A float plane was approaching from the southeast at about one thousand feet. It rapidly overtook them, passing overhead just as Fox Island came into view a mile and half away.

FAT HORSEFLIES BUZZED lazily around the puddled blood of the Justice Department sniper, blood that was already turning dark and sticky on the pine needles of the forest floor. Rigo didn't mind the sound of flies or the smell of spilled blood; he was used to both. He was also used to being around the dead and the near-dead, which was why he hadn't bothered to roll the countersniper's body farther away from the hide.

With the variable-power spotting scope, he searched the curve of shoreline to the east, looking for evidence of opposition foot patrols. As he slowly moved the scope across the landscape, he caught the glint of something among the interwoven tree branches near the water. It wasn't the sunlight reflecting off the water. It looked metallic.

He cranked the magnification power to the maximum. Branches became brown blurs, individual leaves popped into sharp focus and beneath them something moved.

He nudged Alphonso, who pulled back from the sandbagged H&K MSG-90 and peered through the spotting scope.

THE EX-VIETNAM-ERA recon pilot, ex–Bureau of Land Management water bomber pilot, ex-Peru to Colombia coca-base smuggler started his attack run on Fox Island. First he lined up on the center of the house, then he eased down the nose of the plane.

"Now what are you doing?" the Colombian asked, alarmed by the increase in airspeed.

"I'm looking for my dive angle, dipstick," Johnson informed his passenger. "Twelve degrees at five hundred feet of altitude. Otherwise, I guarantee you I ain't gonna hit shit."

As the island's stone-and-timber house grew rapidly before them, four men hopped down from the porch and ran out onto the lawn. They were all dressed in black SWAT outfits and they all had guns. They frantically waved off the plane.

The building rose in front of the windshield until it filled Johnson's homemade rocket sight. He reached for the ignition switch taped to the dash. "I'm going to fly these HEAP birds right through their goddamned front windows," he said.

"Wait! No!" The Colombian seized his wrist as he was about to trigger the launch.

The delay cost Johnson his launch groove.

"Are you nuts or what?" he demanded of his passenger as the shingled roof of the house swept past under them. "Now we're going to have to come around again and maybe get ourselves shot at by a half-dozen machine guns when we make the second pass."

"A new target!" the Colombian told him. "We've been given a new target." He jabbed a finger at the windshield, pointing toward the mainland shore. "There. Dead ahead. See that little notch in the rock at the waterline? It's a cove that's hidden by trees. They want you to hit that with everything you've got."

He saw it, barely. It wasn't much of a cove.

"It's your nickel," Johnson said, throttling up to regain his firing altitude and angle. Actually it was a million nickels.

With the plane diving at twelve degrees, Johnson put the shoreline landmark in his grease-penciled T-LAR—That Looks About Right—sight. He couldn't see anything inside the cove because of the maze of tree trunks and limbs that drooped down into the lake. As they descended, he kept one eye on the altimeter. When it read five hundred feet, he did as he was told and flipped the makeshift firing switch.

Flame and smoke erupted from the tubes, and the plane

shuddered violently as the rockets arced away, leaving white smoke trails in the still air.

BILL RANSOM'S HEADSET crackled as a very angry communications man broke silence. "That goddamned weekend warrior just buzzed the house! He nearly got himself all shot to hell. Get his fucking numbers! At the very least, we're going to have his license."

"Roger, that, Echo. We'll have to wait until he turns, though," Ransom said. "Right now he's coming straight at us. Over."

Ransom didn't see the white smoke puffs under the Cessna's wings. Even if he had, it wouldn't have prepared him for what was about to happen.

The quartet of warheads hammered the narrow, rock-walled cove, shredding the tree cover, the rubber boats and the men inside them. The three SWU men who survived the initial high-explosive blast and shrapnel spray fell stunned and bleeding into the warm water, and there quickly drowned.

THE DRONE of the low-flying float plane froze the eight-man Justice beach patrol. Airspace at this end of the lake was supposed to be restricted to government-use only. They stopped inside the tree line and watched in astonishment as the aircraft dipped and buzzed the safehouse. Then the pilot gunned the engine and pulled the nose up, gaining a couple of hundred feet of altitude in short order.

"Is that guy drunk?" one of the men asked the patrol leader.

"He's going into another dive," the leader said.

Then four rockets streaked away from the high-wing Cessna.

"Jesus! Look!" the patrol leader shouted, pointing at the smoke trails in the sky.

Four almost simultaneous explosions racked the little cove a quarter mile up the curve of beach.

The beach patrol's disbelief turned to horror as falling pieces of trees, boats and men spattered and ringed the smooth surface of the lake.

"Echo! Echo!" the leader shouted into his mike. "This is Charlie."

Even as he spoke, machine guns stuttered down at them from positions higher up the heavily treed slope. Beside him a volley of bullets made solid contact. The man on his right fell to the ground screaming; he had been hit multiple times in the front of both thighs.

"We are under fire!" the patrol leader said into the mike. "Repeat. Echo, we are under fire!"

As he ducked behind a boulder, he saw the muzzle-flashes from behind the trees. They were closing in.

"We've got to make a break. Can we move along the shoreline?" he shouted to the men on either side of him.

The answer came back in 9 mm lead.

Bullets whined overhead, zinging off the big rocks they were hiding behind. Machine-gun fire was coming from three directions now. They'd been outflanked. From the sound of the guns raised against them, they were seriously outnumbered. And their current position wasn't defensible. The patrol leader looked down the hill toward the lake. About thirty-five yards away, a big pile of debris and rock sat on the beach. It wasn't a great choice, but if he waited much longer, they would be encircled.

"Pull back to that logjam!" he ordered his men. "Everybody!"

As they withdrew, dragging their wounded, they fired into the woods above them, sweeping the trees with bullets. Still, two of the patrol never made it to the beach. The return fire from the flanks chopped them down.

The patrol leader was the last man over the log pile.

Slugs gouged and chipped the barkless tree trunk in front of him.

Their position, though improved, was still terrible. With the water to their backs they had nowhere to retreat. They also had no reinforcements, no air cover, no resupply.

"Make your bullets count!" he urged his men.

The patrol leader saw the blur of the hand grenade as it sailed over the top of the logjam. It landed with a soft thud in the sand between him and the water, perfectly placed to nail them all. The leader dropped his weapon and dived out from cover, intending to flip the grenade into the water before it exploded.

He never reached it.

Nine millimeter slugs stitched him from head to foot, sewing him to the soft, warm earth. The frag grenade detonated inches beyond his outstretched fingertips.

The Colombians surged down the hill and overran the smoldering logjam and its devastated occupants. They used their submachine guns at close range to finish off the survivors. Then they directed short bursts of autofire at the house across the lake.

The mainland force stopped shooting when the trio of Outrage boats appeared around the bend of coastline. The Colombians on the beach waved their arms and cheered as the boats cut hard left turns and bore down on the island's north beach.

8

Special Agent Tidman pushed up from his chair as the float plane roared over the house. The wind gust of the low pass shook the timbered rafters.

"What on earth!" he exclaimed.

Eleanor McCullen and Dan Freeberg followed him as he ran to the kitchen. Tidman cracked open the back door in time for all three of them to witness the rocket attack. The sonic boom of the explosions rattled the shuttered kitchen windows in their frames. They watched as the float plane continued unhurriedly on its way. Its wings and fuselage flashed in the sunlight like a silver cross as it gained altitude to clear the tops of the low mountains.

Tidman broke the hollow silence, speaking the words that were on all their minds. "They hit the team at Bravo."

He grabbed a pair of binoculars from the kitchen counter. Optical aids weren't really necessary. The plume of oily smoke rising from the shoreline was visible with the naked eye. A gasoline fire was burning out of control in the little cove.

Then, from across the lake came the back-and-forth crackle of automatic weapons. A firefight had broken out on the mainland.

Through his headset, Tidman was getting the bad news from the observation post-communications center upstairs.

"We intercepted a transmission in Spanish before the plane overflew the house," the comm man told him.

"Sounded like lat-lon coordinates. Could have been a last-second target change."

"What about Bravo?" Tidman said.

"Gone."

"Our snipers?"

"We've lost contact with them, too. And Charlie team just reported they're under attack along the beach and apparently heavily outnumbered. That's the gunfire we're hearing now."

The solid whump of a grenade detonation rolled across the water. More smoke curled up along the shoreline to the east.

"Send out a Mayday," Tidman said, "to any and all law enforcement."

"Yes, sir."

McCullen had only heard half of the conversation. It was enough to scare the daylights out of her. "What does this mean, Alex? How much trouble are we in?" She stood with her back to the big, solid iron cookstove that dominated the lodge's kitchen.

The FBI agent held up a hand and listened once again to the voice through his headphones, then he relayed the information to McCullen and Freeberg.

"We've got three boats coming at us from the north at high speed. They're transporting an estimated two dozen armed hostiles."

A hail of bullets from the far shore pelted the side of the house. With a crash the windows at the far end of the kitchen shattered inward. Nine millimeter slugs clanged into pots and pans hanging on an overhead rack, sending them flying off their hooks. Splinters of wood from the shutters mixed with splinters of glass sprayed across the floor.

"Get down!" Freeberg said, pulling the woman to the floor.

The fusillade continued for several nerve-racking minutes. Then it stopped.

And they heard another engine sound.

"That couldn't be the boats," McCullen said. "Or the plane coming back for another try."

"No," Tidman replied, "that's a helicopter."

Heavy-caliber rifles boomed from the wraparound front porch and the house's upper floor.

THE COLOMBIAN IN THE BOW of the lead boat clutched his chest as the console's Plexiglas window shattered behind him, and he pitched backward into the arms of his surprised countrymen. The .308 slug fired from the island had gone through his torso, through the windshield, nearly taking out the boat's driver, as well.

Gaspar squinted into the spotting scope. "They're shooting at the boats," he told his brother. "There's a gun in the top window on the left. And two are firing from the corner of the porch railing."

Tacho had already set his Leupold scope's BDC for a seven-hundred-yard zero. In its bright view field, he located the top-floor shooter: a shadow behind a cracked shutter. Using the Duplex reticle's Mil Dots, he aimed fifty-four inches low to adjust for his forty-five-degree target angle. Taking up the trigger slack, he waited for the man to fire again. When he saw the muzzle-flash, he broke the trigger. The H&K MSG-90 punched him hard in the shoulder, which was a sensation he thoroughly enjoyed.

It meant death was on its way.

Downrange the Fed was just recovering from his own recoil wave when the 168-grain hollowpoint struck him in the cheek, just below his right eye. The contents of his skull were slung all the way across the room.

"I saw the barrel flip up," Gaspar said. "You got him!"

Tacho swung the scope down to cover the porch and the

two riflemen in black crouching there. They had taken up positions behind the porch roof's heavy wooden supports. In order to shoot at the onrushing boats, the Feds had to bend around the timber beams, exposing themselves to return fire.

The El Salvadoran aimed at the clearer target, using the Mil Dot scale to put the cross hairs twelve inches lower than the man's feet, which would mean a bullet impact roughly in the center of his chest.

Tacho had just begun to tighten down on the trigger when his target jerked back from the post, doubling over at the waist and dropping to his butt. His rifle went skittering across the porch deck.

Rigo had taken the shot.

Tacho swung the Leupold onto the other Fed who knelt behind the porch railing, shouting something at his unmoving partner. Compensating for the angle, Tacho squeezed off a round.

He didn't see what happened because of the recoil. When he recovered the target, the man lay sprawled on the porch.

"Beautiful!" Gaspar cried. "The bullet went right through the railing. See how it's splintered? Right through the railing and into his head."

Sure enough, the section of railing looked like it had been struck by lightning.

Through the scope, Tacho saw the guy twitch, thrash his arms, then roll over. Hardly dead. The hollowpoint bullet had to have fragmented on impact, he thought. The Fed's face was a bloody mess. Splinters from the rail had been driven into his eyes.

Tacho locked on target and prepared to put an end to him.

A small helicopter suddenly appeared over the top of the southern ridge. It flew very fast, skimming the treetops.

As the El Salvadorans watched, the chopper dipped low

over the water, its skids practically throwing a wake, and headed straight for the island. The pilot kept the two-story house between himself and the autofire from the mainland beach.

Whoever he was, he knew what he was doing.

Five feet above the ground and forty yards from the house, the helicopter paused just long enough for a tall man in black with a long satchel slung over his shoulder to step out on a skid and drop to earth. The chopper wheeled away, leaving him, and flew back the way it had come.

The timber-and-stone house protected the new arrival from gunfire coming from the beach to the north, but it didn't block the path of sniper bullets angling down from the mountaintops. The tall man had 120 feet of open ground to cross, and the El Salvadorans had a clear shot at him.

"Brother!" Gaspar exclaimed. "Look who it is! Our old friend, the North American with the cold eyes."

"I'm going to mess him up," Tacho said, snugging the H&K's butt into the hollow of his shoulder. He swung the angle-corrected aim point past the moving figure, using the scope's Mil Dots to take his lead. As he shifted the rifle, he tightened up on the trigger. With machinelike precision, the trigger break and the lead point coincided. The gun bucked as the 168-grain hollowpoint sailed downrange.

9

The moment Bolan and Grimaldi cleared the southern ridge, they knew things had gone sour. On the mainland on the other side of the island, twin spires of smoke climbed lazily into the sky. Over the rotor beat, they could hear the sound of a pitched battle under way. And three white boats crammed with armed landing parties were on a high-speed course for the island's north beach.

"Hang on," Grimaldi said. He dropped the helicopter a sudden one hundred feet and followed the rolling contour of the mountainside as it descended to the lakeshore. Rotor wash lashed the treetops beneath the chopper's skids.

"Drop me on the beach behind the house," Bolan said, reaching back for the grip of the ballistic nylon satchel he had brought with him from Stony Man Farm.

Grimaldi skimmed the helicopter over the surface of the lake. "There are too many of them, Sarge. You can't do it alone. I'll set down and we'll both get out."

"No."

The pilot glanced at his passenger.

"Somebody's got to bring backup and emergency medical," Bolan told him. "That somebody is you, my friend."

The edge in Bolan's voice told Grimaldi that further argument was a complete waste of breath. Keeping the building between himself and the firefight, the Stony Man pilot closed the gap to the LZ. Reaching it, he only hovered four or five seconds.

"Later," Bolan said, stepping out on the skid.

The Executioner landed in a half crouch, protecting the contents of his satchel by holding it firmly against his chest. As the departing helicopter's rotor wash whipped him, he took the bag by the grip and started for the house. The footing was difficult for running. The smooth, silver-dollar-sized beach rocks slid under his weight, slowing him. The bag slowed him, too. Instinctively he knew there was too much open ground to the house's back wall; he would draw fire, for sure. He changed course, almost in midstride. Instead of taking the shortest route, the angle to the wall, he moved straight ahead, parallel to the building.

Something whined over his head, spanging into and scattering the rocks behind him.

The bullet hadn't come from the mainland beach.

The angle was all wrong.

Bolan looked up as he ran. To the right of the house, above its roof line, two mountain peaks loomed from the other side of the lake. A flash came and went on the left-hand peak. So brief, so tiny that a less-experienced man might have thought it an illusion, a trick of the mind under extreme stress. The Executioner knew it was the sun reflecting off a scope lens. The flash burned into his consciousness, as did the other details of the split-second event. He replayed them in his head even as he changed back to his original course to the house.

Upper quarter of the white rock outcrop near the summit. Slightly right of center.

The El Salvadorans were there, seven hundred yards away and as confident as hell. And why not? They could ignore the threat of answering fire from the island below—the people down here were too busy addressing shorter-range targets—and the threat of attack from Justice teams on the mainland had apparently been neutralized.

Fox Island had turned into their own private shooting gallery.

Bolan moved into the cool shadow beside the house. He could hear bullets smacking the other side of the building. Occasional bursts and single shots of return fire were coming from somewhere inside. He shifted the satchel to his left hand and unclipped the Beretta 93-R from its neck lanyard. With the select-fire 9 mm pistol on point ahead of him, he rounded the corner of the house and ran up the stairs to the porch deck.

Two men in black body armor were bent over a fourth figure sprawled on the porch, while a third man knelt by the railing, spraying covering autofire toward the opposite shore. The third man swung the smoking barrel of his Heckler & Koch MP-5 K on Bolan.

For an instant the Fed was going to shoot.

He hadn't seen the chopper land behind the house. He had no way of knowing who the hell the new arrival was. And there was a particularly mean-looking, shoulder-stocked pistol in his right hand. But the Fed didn't shoot. Something about the way the man held himself as he looked death square in the face made the Fed release pressure on the H&K's trigger. It was confidence and authority.

Unquestioned authority.

"Let's get him inside," Bolan said, moving the Beretta to the satchel hand and grabbing the wounded Justice man's leg.

They hurried the fallen man through the house's front door and set him down in a corner of the living room, on the floor beside the fieldstone foundation wall. Another wounded SWU man, hit in the head and face, was being tended to by two men and a woman. Everyone crouched low as bullets zipped through the upper, timbered part of the building's wall.

"Any of you guys Tidman?" Bolan asked.

"Yeah, I'm Tidman," said the man with the headset. The FBI man handed a wad of compression bandages to the woman. "Who the hell are you?"

"I was told you were expecting me."

"You must be the specialist. Great. Only, as you can see, things have come unglued here since you got your flying orders. What we need right now is the Ninth cavalry. Not one guy and a black bag."

"You haven't seen what's in my bag," Bolan said as he looked around the room. It was a shambles—overturned furniture, broken glass, blood. There were six unwounded men in body armor, plus the three civilians.

"I'm McCullen from State," the woman said as she tried to staunch the bleeding from the injured man's eyes.

"Freeberg, DEA," the bald man added.

"Is this everybody?" Bolan said.

"Mitchell's on the back door, off the kitchen," one of the men in body armor replied.

"Our men on the mainland are either dead or out of commission," Tidman added. "We can't expect help from them now."

"In about a minute," Bolan said, "we're going to have three boatloads of armed enemy landing on the beach." He indicated half of the SWU men with a sweep of his hand. "I suggest you three pin them down from these windows. The rest of you come with me to the back door."

The Justice tactical team looked to their boss for confirmation.

"Do it!" Tidman said. He didn't want to surrender command; he had no choice. The situation was out of control. "Do every goddamned thing he tells you."

Picking up his satchel and his Beretta, Bolan did a quick survey of the rooms leading to the kitchen. He found nothing of value to him. When he reached the kitchen, he directed the Justice men past him toward the door.

"Here they come!" Mitchell announced, ducking back into the room. "They're driving the boats right up on the beach!"

"Pin them down," Bolan said. "Don't let them advance on us."

"Who is that guy?" Mitchell asked the others as they punched the remaining glass from the windows over the sink and pushed open the shutters. "And what the hell is he doing?"

Bolan had put down his weapon and his bag and was examining the huge, plate-iron, cookstove. Covering the four large holes machined into the top of the cooking surface were heavy metal disks the size of pie tins. They swung out of the way on single steel hinge pins. He opened the oven door, bent down and looked inside.

Behind him, from the windows and back door, guns blazed in short full-auto bursts. Cartridge casings clattered on the floor and chimed in the porcelain sink.

Beside the stove was a firebox filled with short lengths of dry wood. Beside that was a double-bladed ax. Bolan picked up the ax and took a home-run swing at the stove-pipe, aiming at the base where it connected to the stove. The blade sparked on the pipe as it cut through, soot and dust billowing from the broken chimney.

At the same instant, a volley of returned fire from the beached boats swept the windows and door, forcing the SWU men to duck below the line of the stone wall.

Kneeling there, they all stared up at him like he was out of his mind.

"Help me move this thing," he said.

It took three of them and Bolan to drag the stove to the living room. Its iron clawfeet gouged inch-deep furrows in the hardwood floors. At Bolan's direction they turned the stove in the front doorway, so the oven door faced the house, then they pushed it over and out. It crashed to its side on the deck.

"Get back into position," Bolan told the three men.

"I hope you know what you're doing," Freeberg said, speaking to the rear of the Executioner's head as he bent over his long black satchel.

Bolan pulled out a set of earmuff-style hearing protectors and a pair of clear plastic goggles.

From a silicone-treated gun sock, he removed his countersniper weapon of choice. It was an H. S. Precision-stocked M-24 Sniping System built around a Konzaki-customized Remington Model 700 action. The long gun was chambered in .300 Winchester Magnum and topped with a Leupold M-3 10× sniper scope.

Donning the ear protectors and the goggles, Bolan climbed through the oven door, putting half of his body into the oven.

Inside the iron box, he shifted one of the hinged metal plates aside, edging it far enough out of the way so he could poke his rifle barrel through the bottom of the gap. By sliding the gun forward to the forestock, he was able to push the plate back and clear his scope field. Using the stove's two topmost holes, he had a 120-degree view of the beach.

Two of the three Outrage boats had been driven onto shore. With their deep-V bows stuck up in the air, they presented the sides of their fiberglass hulls to him. From inside and behind the two boats, two-dozen crouching men fired autoweapons at the house. Smoke from the gunfire drifted back over the lake. The third boat was beached less completely than the others, and because of its angle to the house, it was partially hidden behind its sister boats. No one was shooting from behind it. The Colombians had all moved up to the front boats as they prepared to charge and overrun the house.

As soon as they saw the barrel of Bolan's Remington pop out of the stove top, they started directing fire at him.

Their FMJ 9 mm rounds clanged and pinged off the heavy cast-iron stove top.

No way, Bolan thought.

The bullet impacts knocked flakes of rust and encrusted food ash off the inside of the oven.

Nothing more.

He settled down behind the scope, adjusting the BDC for a one-hundred-yard zero. Using the reticle's Mil Dots to compensate for the actual fifty-five-yard distance to the boats, he took aim at the side of the nearest boat where he had seen a man just duck.

The Remington bellowed, and the heavy recoil made its barrel scour against the edge of the iron plate, leaving the beautiful deep blueing of its steel behind.

The 200-grain boattail softpoint slipped through the vessel's fiberglass-and-foam hull like it was nothing. Then it passed through the man's torso, turning his insides to unrecognizable mush. The slug's horrendous impact hurled him backward across the deck.

Recovering from the recoil wave, Bolan caught the briefest glimpse of the soles of the man's shoes as he toppled over the far bow rail. He thumbed the rust and ash from his goggles, then chambered another live round. He moved his aim point aft a couple of yards and fired again.

Again the powerful bullet found no obstacle in its path that it could not overcome, taking out an enemy gunner.

After the third shot, Bolan could hear the Colombians screaming. They were doing more screaming than shooting. It had begun to dawn on them that their cover was no cover at all when the opposition was shooting a .300 Winchester Magnum. Hurriedly some of them withdrew to hide behind the second, more distant boat. Bolan ejected the spent case and locked the bolt down on a fresh round.

As he pulled the stock's spot weld to his cheek, the stove clanged with a much heavier impact—a .308, then another clang, same caliber.

The El Salvadorans had found the range.

The problem was, the range was too long.

Even though the 168-grain rifle bullets the snipers were firing had considerably more power than the 115-grain pistol rounds their comrades behind the Whaler boats were using, they started to run out of velocity after six hundred yards. From a distance of seven hundred yards, the 7.62 mm slugs might dent, but no way could they penetrate the stove's outer wall.

All the snipers' shots accomplished was to remind the Executioner of their existence.

He fired another round at the closest vessel, putting the bullet through its built-in gas tank. The nineteen-foot boat was lifted off the ground by the force of the detonating fuel. Its hull sheered into a half-dozen large, "unsinkable" sections, and millions of tiny, sinkable fragments. Burning fuel and debris, fiberglass and human, showered the men hiding behind the nearest boat.

Bolan shifted position inside the stove, prying back the other view port. Looking through the scope, he found the outcrop of white rock, set up his BDC for the distance, then searched the boulders for the sniper hide. There were lots of likely places, and it would have taken him longer if he hadn't already known where to look.

Upper quarter, slightly off center.

The El Salvadorans appeared in outline, human-shaped shadows, head and shoulders only, low over the top of a flat boulder. He couldn't tell which one was the sniper and which the spotter. Bolan assumed they were standing in a cleft or depression in the rock face. Behind them was a sheer rock wall.

Adjusting for the up-angled shot, he aimed for the man

who was the most exposed. He didn't rush. He was in no hurry. The surviving men on the beach, though numerous, were in total disarray. He had a minute or two to spend. He let his heart rate slow, then he fell into the right breathing rhythm. Steady, measured rises and falls.

In the scope's view field he saw his target's head move slightly. Probably getting back behind the gun or the spotting scope, the Executioner thought. He took up the trigger slack and, when everything was right, he applied a fraction more pressure to it. It snapped back under his fingertip, and the 200-grain bullet roared away.

He didn't have time to spot the shot.

Somebody was pulling on his foot. He cracked back one of his ear protectors.

"Hey, the bastards are turnin' tail!" one of the SWU men shouted at him.

Bolan could hear the big engine's roar. He poked his weapon out the other view port. Sure enough, the rearmost boat was climbing up on plane and turning away from the beach. There were only two guys behind the console, though; the rest of the Colombians had to still be on the beach.

The Executioner looked over the scope at the remaining intact boat.

It, too, had moved.

By pushing the boat from the far side, and pulling on the mooring lines from the rear, the dozen or so Colombians had managed to back it off the rocks and into water deep enough to float it. They had turned the boat so the bow faced him. They were all clumped together, hiding behind the stern—keeping nineteen feet of hull between them and the next 200-grain softpoint round. They hadn't gotten the outboard started yet.

They could wait, then, Bolan thought, pulling the ear protector back down.

He clicked the Leupold's BDC to a new zero. When the escaping boat was two hundred yards away, he swung the cross hairs on target and then through it to take his lead.

The Remington thumped his shoulder, hard.

10

Francisco "The Tactician" Verdusco pounded down the Outrage boat's binnacle throttle control with a single blow of his balled fist. The 250-horse Yamaha engine responded with a surge of power. The vessel jumped from zero to sixty-five miles per hour so quickly that it threw the Tactician's second-in-command, Raul Sinblanca, facefirst into the front of the howling Yamaha's engine cowl.

He was lucky he didn't fly over the stern because Verdusco would have let him drown.

"Come on!" the Tactician yelled back at him. "Get up here!"

Sinblanca crawled forward until he could get a grip on the leaning post, then he pulled himself up.

"Now, hang on!" Verdusco told him. He had no intention of slowing down for his passenger's comfort or safety.

Sinblanca assumed a two-handed, white-knuckled grip on the console's stainless-steel railing.

Steering with one hand, Verdusco keyed the hand-held transmitter on the console's dash. "Ramon! This is Francisco," he shouted into the built-in mike. "Meet me at the easternmost beach fire. I want everyone there but the snipers. And don't forget the grenades!"

Suddenly Sinblanca slammed into him so hard that the steering wheel was momentarily knocked to the left.

The console's smoke gray plexiglas dash cover exploded, as did the majority of Sinblanca's guts.

The boat's sickening yaw hurled Verdusco across the console, and it took all his strength to recover the helm. When he had, he looked down at shredded intestines on the outside of his comrade's shirtfront. The man was stone dead.

"Bastard!" he swore, dropping on one knee, keeping his entire body below the top of the leaning post. Beside him, Sinblanca's blood ran down the fiberglass deck's splash gutter and into the stern sump.

Whoever was sniping from the house was damned good. Too damned good.

Verdusco could steer with a hand on the bottom of the wheel, but he couldn't see where he was going because the console was in the way. He had to gauge his progress across the lake by swinging the bow back and forth, and looking off to port, then starboard.

He rose from his knees only when he was within a stone's throw of the mainland shore. It was then he discovered that he had missed the rendezvous point by a quarter mile. He cut a foaming turn and when he reached the logjam fire, he drove the bow onto the beach where a dozen more men waited.

"Get in!" the Tactician ordered them even as he dumped Sinblanca's corpse over the side into the shallows. When they paused, he shouted at them, "Quick! Quick!"

Ramon was the first on board. He carried a canvas satchel full of fragmentation grenades. "Something has happened to the Ruiz brothers," he told the drug lord's field general.

"What do you mean 'something'? Don't you know what?"

"Whoever was on the transmitter up there was incoherent, boss," Ramon said. "Crying. Yelling. I couldn't tell what happened or which one it happened to. But it must've been real bad. Whoever it was on the transmitter, he said he was coming down from the mountain and he wanted to cross over and fight on the island with us.''

"Is he crazy? We don't have time to wait for anyone," Verdusco said. "We've got to tighten the noose and end this before help appears. I need all my snipers to stay in place."

While the men clambered into the boat, he used the transmitter to try to raise the Ruiz brothers. He got no answer to his code signal. A call to Rigo and Alphonso on the other mountaintop was successful, however.

"We're going to either kill them in the house," he told Rigo, "or drive them out to you. Be ready! And don't miss!"

He threw the transmitter back on the blood-spattered console. Ordering all the men to the stern, he shifted the weight distribution enough so he could use the outboard to reverse the boat off the beach. Then he started a wide arc that would keep the boat well out of effective sniper range, and eventually bring them to the south side of the island.

"IT ISN'T A RETREAT," Bolan said, "it's a reinforcement. Look for yourself." He handed the binoculars to Tidman.

The FBI agent scanned the far shore, then passed the binoculars to Eleanor McCullen. "What the hell are we going to do?" he said. "We've got support in the air to us right now, but they're not going to make it in time, are they?"

Bolan didn't answer directly. "I can take out the boat on this side," he said, indicating the vessel still drifting off the north shore, "but I can't guarantee there won't be survivors left to back the other boat's play when it arrives. My guess is, they're going to try and squeeze us, attacking from north and south simultaneously. They figure we don't have enough guns or ammo to keep them off."

"Maybe they're right," Tidman said. "We lost three

more men in the last exchange. That brings us down to seven, counting everybody.''

"Which leaves about three people to defend each side of the house," Freeberg said. "Three against a dozen or more. That's fairly crummy odds in my book.''

"We've still got the helicopter," Tidman declared. "They haven't shot it up yet. And Mitchell can fly it.''

"We can't all bail out," Bolan told him. "If we do, none of us will survive. Think about it. As soon as they see us piling into the chopper, they're going to come running and unload everything they have at it. We probably wouldn't even get off the ground.''

"That's a pretty pessimistic view," Freeberg said.

"Realistic," Bolan corrected him.

"I don't see that there is any choice left to us," Tidman said. "If we stay here, it's a certainty that we'll all die. If some of us try to fly out, they might make it.''

"You want somebody to stay behind and provide covering fire?" McCullen asked. "Talk about rough duty!''

"There's a good chance," Tidman went on, "that if we—meaning you, Dan, Mitchell and I—either get away or die trying, the bastards will be satisfied and withdraw.''

"I can't say what those scumbags are going to do, sir," one of the surviving SWU men said, "and I can't honestly say I care much, either. If you're asking for volunteers, count me in. I lost most of my closest friends here today, and I'll be goddamned if I leave this stinking pile of rock with an unfired round in my gun.''

The other surviving SWU man nodded in agreement.

"I don't think the fly-out is the right decision," Bolan said. "If we hunker down, we can probably hold them off until help arrives.''

"I think we've discarded that option," Tidman said.

"In that case," Bolan replied, "I don't have a problem with hanging around here, either.''

"Go and replace Mitchell on the back door," Tidman told one of the SWU men. "He needs to preflight the chopper right now."

"And I'm going to try and lower the odds a bit," Bolan said. He laid his Remington on a sofa cushion and opened up the black satchel. From inside another silicon-impregnated gun sock he removed an M-16 A-1 equipped with an M-203 grenade launcher. He took three 40 mm high-explosive grenades from the satchel's interior bandolier.

"Couldn't you have used that thing before?" McCullen asked him.

Bolan pushed down on the M-203's barrel latch and slid the barrel forward. "I could have but it would have been risky—they were too close to the house," he said, feeding a grenade into the breech. "Now they're not."

He moved to the kitchen and took a quick look over the window ledge above the sink, then he ducked back down. The boat had drifted about one hundred yards from shore. It still faced the house, bow forward. If the Colombians were hiding inside, they were keeping well down. They also might have been in the water, hanging on to the mooring lines and the engine. They could have been standing on the lake bottom, too. From where he was standing, there was no way of telling.

And it really didn't matter.

He pushed the M-203's safety forward, releasing it, then rose and turned. As the M-16's buttstock slid against his shoulder, he located the target over the sight leaf. He launched the HE round through the glassless window frame and dropped down, keeping his eyes just above the level of the frame. He watched for the grenade's impact point in case a range adjustment on a second shot was needed.

It wasn't.

The 40 mm grenade thunderclapped, lighting up the Outrage boat like the Fourth of July. The boat flashed white as it flew apart, then red-orange as it blazed. Burning fuel swept across the water's surface. As the fires ebbed back and forth, he could see a half-dozen bodies floating face-down in the lake.

That was a half dozen fewer to worry about.

TACHO RUIZ RAN screaming down the mountain.

He wasn't screaming with terror; he was screaming with rage.

What had happened was impossible to believe, and yet it was as undeniable as the blood that still dripped from Tacho's face, that soaked the front of his T-shirt.

His brother's blood.

They had been laughing about the North American hiding in the old stove. Tacho had hit the stove with a rifle bullet, and the clang had echoed back to them across the lake. Gaspar had said the noise inside the stove would permanently cross the cold one's blue eyes for him. He even crossed his own eyes to demonstrate the effect.

They were laughing over that, then Gaspar reared up from the ledge and slammed into the rock wall behind them. He fell forward, back onto the ledge, arms limp, chin resting on the flat stone.

Tacho had suddenly realized his face and hair were wet. When he wiped his eyes, he saw it was blood. He looked at his brother, and his heart stopped. Gaspar's eyes had popped out of their sockets, and the back of his head was gone. From the base of his skull all the way to his eye-brows, there was an empty crater. No, worse than a cra-ter—it was a cirque. Blood from his severed neck arteries jetted high in the air, geysering up out of the awful emp-tiness where his brain had been.

Tacho couldn't bring himself to touch his brother's corpse. That ruined shell wasn't Gaspar. Pain swelled in his chest, as if half his own heart had been torn away by the blue-eyed man's bullet.

The North American, who was still alive across the water.

The idea that the others might kill the man buzzed in his head like a stinging insect. It couldn't be allowed to happen. Revenge had to be his. He couldn't stay on the mountain.

Tacho picked up the transmitter and punched in Ramon's call code with a shaking hand. When the man answered, Tacho could barely talk and he couldn't make himself understood. The harder he tried, the more emotional he got.

"Wait!" he said finally. "Wait for me!"

He threw down the transmitter and, grabbing his rifle, took off down the mountain.

"I will kill your murderer, Gaspar!" he shouted as he ran. "I promise you. I will slit his belly open and drink his blood!"

He fell and got up many times as he descended the wooded slope. In the process he cut his hands, his knees, his face. His blood and Gaspar's mixed. When he finally stumbled, gasping, onto the beach, he saw the boat and all the Colombian soldiers speeding away from him, down the shore.

"No!" he cried. "Come back!"

They weren't coming back.

They had left him behind, robbed him of his due.

He charged into the water, screaming. Waist deep, he flailed with his arms and with the rifle. Tacho couldn't swim. If he could have, he would have crossed the lake by himself, powered by the insane blood lust that boiled inside him.

He shouldered the H&K and without really aiming—he couldn't aim for his tears—he fired shot after shot at the island. And after every futile discharge, he snarled, "Die, you bastard, die!"

THE EXPLOSION that destroyed the other Outrage boat turned every head in Verdusco's vessel. A pyre of flame and column of oily, black smoke was all that remained of the sister boat and crew.

"Son of a bitch!" the Tactician fumed, yanking the engine out of gear.

"Now what?" Ramon asked.

They drifted for a few seconds while Verdusco stood rigid, eyes tightly shut, as if turned to stone. The whine of the helicopter's turbines starting up snapped him out of it.

"Boss, they're going to escape," Ramon said.

"No, they aren't," Verdusco replied. "I want the four strongest men in the bow with hand grenades." As Ramon picked out the men, Verdusco added, "Don't pull the pins until we are on the beach."

With that, he slipped the engine back into gear and made a hard right turn for the island. He could see the helicopter's rotors spinning, faster and faster, becoming a blur. He pounded down the throttle.

THROUGH THE SPOTTING scope, Alphonso saw the man run from the house to the helicopter. It was what they had been waiting for.

"Look!" he said, nudging his partner's shoulder.

"I see him," Rigo replied without taking his eye from the H&K's telescopic sight.

Alphonso put aside the spotting scope and picked up his M-1 A-1. There would be no spotter on this shoot. The entire mission now depended on their two guns, on their placing as many rounds as possible through the front of the helicopter's Plexiglas bubble.

When Alphonso found the pilot in his scope's view field,

the man was inside the chopper, already cranking up the turbines.

That everything hung on his marksmanship didn't rattle the El Salvadoran one bit. He was supremely confident in his abilities. And more important than the size of his ego, the two of them had fired twenty-five to thirty rounds apiece down at the target area. In his little spiral notebook, Alphonso had jotted down scope settings and wind-drift allowances for every shot he had taken. Rigo had done the same. Both men referred to these pencil notations and made final, fine adjustments to their rifles' sights.

Alphonso swung his scope from the helicopter to the house's front door. There was some activity going on inside the doorway. Shadowy forms were moving about. "They're getting ready to make a break for it," he said. "When do we start?"

"Wait until they're all strapped in," Rigo answered. "That way, even if we miss on the first shots, it will take them a few seconds to unbuckle and get out the doors. It will give us time to follow up before they clear the chopper."

"REMIND THAT PILOT of yours to turn south as soon as he gets airborne," Bolan told Tidman. "Otherwise, he'll be flying you right into those snipers' guns."

"Hey, there are no words..." Eleanor McCullen said, reaching out to touch his hand.

"Ditto," Dan Freeberg added.

"Yeah, I know," Bolan said. "Just keep your heads down."

"You, too," Tidman said.

All three of the soon-to-be-departing passengers braced themselves by the front door of the house. They had donned body armor stripped from the fallen SWU men.

Across the short stretch of open beach, the pilot, Mitchell, raised his hand, giving them the go-ahead. The bird was ready to fly.

Tidman, McCullen and Freeberg dashed for the helicopter, ducking low to avoid the rotors.

On the other side of the helicopter, Bolan could see the last Outrage boat bearing down on them at a range of about 250 yards. He pushed off the M-203's safety and lobbed an HE air-burst grenade high over the beach, dropping it in front of the onrushing boat.

The 40 mm shell exploded five feet above the water, sending shards of razor-sharp steel wire flying in all directions. The boat swerved but kept on coming. The shell had fallen short.

As Bolan reloaded for another try, the three passengers clambered into the helicopter. They were no sooner in their seats than the pilot throttled up and lifted off.

The chopper rose fifteen feet straight up, then hung there for a split second.

A split second was too long.

Bullets whacked into the front of the Plexiglas canopy. Bolan could see Mitchell jerk at the impacts, hit twice. The helicopter shifted in space, slewing to the right, dipping its rotor on that side.

McCullen turned toward him. On the other side of the window he could see her face. She was screaming.

Two more shots fractured the chopper's windshield, and it dropped from the sky.

Its rotor tips touched the beach and flew apart, then the body of the machine crashed down flat on its skids. The canopy bubble sheered clear of the frame, leaving Tidman unprotected in the copilot's chair. As the FBI agent clawed at his seat belt, Bolan autofired the M-16 at the twin peaks, emptying the 40-round magazine. He was trying to forestall the inevitable.

Tidman convulsed in his seat as a bullet slammed into the front of his throat.

In the same instant, Bolan caught a whiff of spilled aviation gas and saw the electrical system arcing.

Then the helicopter burst into a ball of flame.

Still strapped in the back seats, their bodies writhing, McCullen and Freeberg died horribly.

There was nothing the Executioner could do.

11

Deborah Ailes caught herself on the verge of gushing to the young man in glasses sitting on the other side of the stretch limousine. She blushed to the roots of her shoulder-length red hair. Gushing, not blushing, was probably her most serious professional flaw.

She had been told that by Ashley Rossignol, the sleek, leggy brunette who occupied the limo seat beside the Northwest computer-software tycoon. Rossignol was Ailes's mentor, her broker-guru. Rossignol owned Plantation Cay Realty, for whom Ailes was a blossoming agent-in-training.

The redhead had also been warned about gushing at her real-estate-license exam seminar. The videotape sales simulation had highlighted the problem for her, and the three-person video-evaluation panel had been most emphatic: clients didn't trust agents whose closing pitch was so sticky it gave them cavities.

The trouble right now was that Ailes was excited. And when she was excited, she tended to gush.

Inside the velvet-upholstered cabin of the limo, she and Rossignol circled Wayne Witter like a pair of Chanel-scented great white sharks. The deal for the Mahoney estate was all but done. They had just finished a highly cordial—and extravagantly expensive—meal at La Principessa, Plantation Cay's newest and most exclusive restaurant, with Rupert Mahoney himself. And now they were on their way to a final night walk through house and grounds. If everything went smoothly, and there was no reason to doubt that it would, in less than twenty-four hours the brokerage firm would collect about a million dollars in fees and commissions. Some small part of that huge sum would go to Deborah Ailes, enough for her to live well on for a long time.

It didn't take many home sales on Plantation Cay to make an agent a mid-six-figure annual income. The island was owned and inhabited solely by the very rich and their hired help. It was totally secure. Every estate had its own private white sand beaches and private docks with deep-water moorage. While, across the water, the Miami skyline was visible from every land parcel, the surrounding estates weren't. The estates were encircled by high walls and protected by armed private security patrols. There had never been a successful robbery on the Cay, which said something about the effectiveness of the security. The people who owned the island were accustomed to the best in service in every area of their lives.

Service, Rossignol had told Ailes a hundred times, was what selling real estate was all about.

Rupert Mahoney actually spent very little time at the Cay. It was, however, often full of guests. When she had toured the place earlier in the week with Mr. Witter, more than a dozen Hispanic men rested in the lounge chairs around the Olympic-sized outdoor pool. South Americans, she had been told. It seemed that Mahoney did much of his business or had major investments down there, it wasn't clear which.

When Ailes had seen all the Latin guys, the first thing she thought was drug dealers. It was only natural, it being Florida and their coming from south of the border, cocaine country. But Mahoney appeared the very opposite of a drug person. He was deeply tanned with close-cropped steel gray hair, thin, tall and athletic; he looked like the professional yachtsman he was. And even more than his outward appearance, Mr. Mahoney's low-key yet forceful manner inspired her every confidence.

Though none of the men had said anything to her as she walked around the pool, she had felt their eyes crawling all over her. The sexual tension had been most thrilling. And gratifying. Ailes had not only recently graduated from real-estate school, but she had also graduated from a nationally syndicated weight-loss-and-exercise program. In a six-week, complete mind-and-body makeover, she had gained a profession and dropped thirty pounds of ugly fat. She still thought of herself as a teensy bit heavy and soft in the tush, but those sexy South Americans didn't seem to notice. And she'd always had a cute face. Not sophisticated and sensual like Rossignol's, but bright and happy, like a beautifully wrapped Christmas present. It was a look that her mentor said could make her a lot of commission money on Plantation Cay.

Rossignol was saying something to Mr. Witter about wintering on the Cay, name-dropping the former politicians and movie stars who habitually spent Thanksgiving through New Year's there. The computer billionaire seemed less interested in his potential neighbors than in the way Rossignol was "accidentally" brushing his thigh with hers. Ailes knew she wasn't coming on to him because the woman had explained the technique. It was much more subtle than a straightforward offer of sex. She had called it the "touchy-feelie-friendly" close. It was meant to confuse the buyer at a critical moment in the deal. To return to the animal analogy: the great white shark smelled blood in the water and circled tighter, the narrowing spirals diverting the victim's attention, upsetting his equilibrium, short-circuiting his instinct to flee, turning panic into paralysis.

Chomp-chomp.

The limo turned into the estate's redbrick, palm-lined driveway to the heavy front gate. From the security kiosk on the other side, a uniformed, armed gateman looked them over, then hit the switch that drew back the steel barrier. As they rolled past the entrance, Ailes saw two more men, these not in gray-on-black uniforms, but in expensive suit jackets. They were carrying what looked like very small machine guns on black straps that went over their shoulders. Probably some kind of special security people, she thought. Maybe even Mr. Mahoney's traveling team of bodyguards.

The Mahoney mansion was a Florida art deco masterpiece: a sprawling, pastel-stucco and panoramic-glass confection, surrounded by splashing, multitiered fountains. Lit up at night, it looked like a gigantic sugar cake.

Atop the broad, numerous entry steps, on either side of the double-doorway arch, stood several more well-dressed South Americans. They were also carrying stubby black guns on shoulder straps. They seemed very relaxed and happy, as did Mr. Mahoney when he came out to greet them.

"Witter, come on in," he said, putting an arm around the younger man's shoulders. "I want you to poke around here as long as you like. If you need or want anything, ask anybody you see and they'll help you."

Ailes and Rossignol had been through the mansion so many times in the past month they knew the place by heart. As Mr. Mahoney explained some of the huge French Impressionist paintings to their new owner—he was selling the place and its contents—Ailes wondered, and not for the first time, why there was no Mrs. Mahoney in residence. She had never seen a woman hanging on his arm. She had never seen a man, either, but that didn't prove anything.

Wayne Witter lasted only fifteen minutes of the home tour before he threw in the towel. He was too drunk to continue. He had already decided to sign on the dotted line, anyway. He told them as much as they packed him back into the limousine.

When Rossignol and Ailes started to get in the limo with him, Mahoney took a gentle but firm grip on their arms just above the elbows. "Hey, where are you two going?" he asked.

"Back to the hotel," Rossignol said. She didn't struggle in his grasp, but clearly she wasn't comfortable being held that way.

"Stay," Mahoney told her through a broad, confidence-inspiring smile. "Stay and help us celebrate the sale. We've got a party planned."

The woman immediately tried to make excuses. "We'd love to, Rupert, we really would, but we already promised to take Mr. Witter back to his hotel suite, and there are a few little things we still have to discuss with him before money changes hands tomorrow."

"You're going to discuss business with a guy in that state?" Mahoney scoffed. "Stay. We need you. We're a little out of balance, boy-girl."

When Rossignol still resisted, Mahoney laid down the law. "I'm not going to take no for an answer," he said. "You two have worked real hard up to this point. It's time for some fun. Don't let me down now."

The woman relented, but only just.

"We'd like to freshen up, in that case," she said. There was an edge of resignation in her voice, almost defeat, which Ailes had never heard from her before.

"Of course," Mahoney said. "You'll find everyone in the ballroom. You know where that is."

The two women retreated to one of the mansion's lavish, white marble bathrooms. Their high heels clicked as they crossed the highly polished stone floor. Ailes hummed as she began to do a little touch-up work with her lipstick.

Her companion wasn't the least bit happy as she examined her face in the mirror above the hand-painted, gold-leaf-edged porcelain sinks.

"Is something wrong?" Ailes asked her with concern. "Is there a problem with the deal that I don't know about? Do you have a headache? Are you too tired for a party?"

"I'm *always* too tired for this kind of party," the woman replied, her tone highly irritated.

Seeing the thoroughly puzzled expression on Ailes's face, the broker stopped rummaging deep into inner recesses of her handbag and clarified things for her.

"I hope you brought your diaphragm along, Deb. Otherwise, you're never going to know who the father was."

FRANCISCO VERDUSCO opened the storeroom door a crack. Tacho Ruiz lay on his back on a mattress on the concrete floor. He was clad in his briefs and the El Salvadoran's head was lolled back, his mouth slack, his terrible pointed teeth showing between parted lips. Tacho's hard, muscular chest rose and fell, his breathing slow and deep. From the doorway, Verdusco could see the fresh bruises on his face, arms and body, bruises delivered by the five men it had taken to restrain him for the doctor.

"Shouldn't we rebind his hands and feet?" Verdusco asked the Colombian-born physician. "What if he wakes up?"

"He isn't going to wake up for eight or ten hours," the doctor assured him. "I've given him the chemical equivalent of a straitjacket. He's so loaded he's practically comatose. And I'll be back down to look in on him every three or four hours, long before it wears off."

The physician put a hand on Verdusco's shoulder. "Don't worry about your friend," he said. "He's suffering from some terrible emotional shock, but he looks young and healthy. I'm sure he'll recover just fine, given time and proper medication and attention.''

Verdusco scratched his head. He wasn't at all sure. "It's the twin thing," he said. "To lose a twin brother must be most awful."

"I suppose so. I wouldn't know."

The doctor glanced toward the stairway leading up to the main floor. The sounds of loud dance music were drifting down to them, and he was eager to get back to the festivities.

Verdusco closed the storeroom door. There wasn't much point in trying to go over the details about the Ruiz brothers with the doctor, how the other brother had died in front of this one's eyes, what they did for a living, what the surviving brother was capable of. These were things that the doctor didn't need to know, and probably didn't want to know.

Based on the evidence of the past few hours, Verdusco was afraid that Tacho's mind had completely snapped, that he was no longer controllable—that in fact the most merciful and safest thing to do would be to put a .380 hollowpoint slug behind his ear while he peacefully slept.

It had been a lucky thing for Verdusco that the El Salvadoran had run out of bullets by the time they returned to the beach to retrieve him. He had no doubt that Tacho would've shot him dead.

Wild-eyed, his face caked with congealing gore, Tacho had set upon poor, unprepared Ramon, who happened to be the first to step off onto the beach. Before they could pull Tacho off, he had sunk his jagged teeth into Ramon's throat. A ragged chunk of skin came away when they dragged him free, but he had cut no major blood vessels in the man's neck—the fangs had slid over the muscle and tendon.

It was a serious wound, however. And one that would leave a horrible scar.

There had been no question about saving the torn flesh for later regrafting.

Tacho had swallowed it.

Verdusco's hand dipped inside his front waistband, his fingers touching the butt of the little semiautomatic pistol he kept holstered there.

No, he'd better wait, he thought, sleep on it and make the final decision the following day. If Tacho showed any improvement at all, he would stay the execution indefinitely. The truth was, Verdusco hated to lose a man of such special talent. And he knew that his boss, Raffi del Borgo, had also held the Ruiz brothers in the highest esteem.

He shut the hasp and dropped the door's padlock in place. He didn't click the lock shut because there was only one key for it, and because the lock's tempered-steel shank was sufficient to hold the door closed and keep the room's deranged occupant safely inside. "After you," he said, directing the doctor up the stairs.

In the ballroom the party was well under way. When the doctor opened the door, Verdusco got a glimpse of men and women—whores specially imported for the night—laughing and drinking. The party was a special little bonus for the hit crews. Del Borgo was very pleased by the speedy and thorough way they had handled the job.

The following day, after the escrow on the estate closed, all the Colombian soldiers, including Verdusco, were going to be paid in full for their services. And the widows and orphans of the men who had died in the operation would be paid in full, too. Del Borgo had promised that when the deal was made. It was the least he could do for them.

"Aren't you coming in?" the doctor said, holding the door open for him.

"I have other duties, unfortunately," he answered. "Enjoy yourself."

Verdusco continued down the long, wide hallway. The duties he referred to involved escorting del Borgo and his live-in, blond whore back to Ocala in the helicopter. Missing the party wasn't a sacrifice for him. He was too old for the all-night sex. He much preferred to be with just one woman at a time, either his new young wife or his well-trained mistress of five years. Most of all, he didn't want to show his age to the young turks he commanded. He didn't want them to know that he couldn't keep up anymore. The Colombian street soldiers screwed like a warren of jackrabbits, trying to outdo one another.

The whores would earn their money tonight on Plantation Cay.

12

Brenda Lee Baker felt the familiar, uncomfortable lurch in the pit of her stomach as the helicopter lifted off the Plantation Cay pad. The pilot flew east, turning over the dark Atlantic as he gained altitude. The lights of Miami swung around in front of them on the horizon as they reached cruising altitude over the bay, and in a few minutes the city unrolled beneath them.

Del Borgo leaned over close to her and said, "You seem very quiet tonight. Is everything all right?"

"I'm fine."

He gave her a searching look. "You aren't acting like you're fine. You insist on coming all the way down here with me, then decide you don't want to eat at La Principessa, after all."

"I just changed my mind. I wasn't hungry."

"Too bad. You missed the chance to meet the estate agents. They would've amused you. Of course, you would've seen through them at once. They are occasional dabblers in your profession, when the business situation calls for it. I think their amateur status is going to be in some jeopardy tonight. They are about to have their baptism by fire, so to speak."

If you played with fire, you got burned, Baker thought. She had no sympathy for part-time whores with hokey "professional" diplomas that allowed them to pretend they weren't actually selling their tails to make a paycheck.

"Come on," del Borgo said. "Something's bothering you. Is it the El Salvadoran colonel? You didn't arrange to come with me in order to get away from him, did you?"

Baker had been dreading this moment. As the Colombian's highly paid, full-time employee, she was supposed to do what he told her—which translated into sleeping with whomever he wanted her to, no questions asked. Del Borgo wasn't stupid; she had known he would figure it out. She'd decided that, weighing the two risks—his anger, and the Salvadoran's perverted brutality— that she would take her chances with del Borgo.

"The man is worse than a pig," she said.

"You don't like sleeping with him, I take it?"

"I don't like being in the same state as him."

Del Borgo twisted his ring, testing the hard, sharp edges of the green stone against the pads of his fingers. "You are afraid of him."

Colonel Suarez scared the living hell out of her, but she was too proud, and too smart, to admit that to the drug lord. Baker looked him straight in the eye and said, "The only man I'm afraid of is you."

Del Borgo smiled. He liked that answer.

"I appreciate that this has been a particularly difficult job for you," he said. "I have rarely asked you to provide services to someone I do not respect. Once, maybe twice before this. For your extra effort, I'll give you a nice bonus, over and above your salary."

His eyes grew distant, and he shook his head. "In many ways these El Salvadorans resemble wild dogs. They are useful under certain conditions, but mostly they are a big pain in the ass. If you don't keep them tightly chained, they will bite you. It is in their nature to be vicious and unreasoning. At any rate I felt it necessary to keep this particular mongrel completely occupied. I didn't want him interfering with events that he had no part in. Those events are now complete, so I have no more reason to consider him. And you have nothing more to fear. He is about to leave."

"The U.S.?"

"No, Brenda," he said, turning his ring. "This earth."

TREADING WATER, Mack Bolan watched the helicopter pass overhead. It was already too high for him to feel its rotor wash. The people in the chopper had narrowly escaped with their lives. He knew there was a chance that his primary target, Raffi del Borgo, was aboard.

It changed nothing.

He was committed to a hardstrike against the drug lord's empire this night, a payback for what had happened at Lake Margaret. He could still see the woman from State writhing in flames. And he could still taste, with anger, his own helplessness at that moment.

Until now Bolan had been fighting a defensive battle, forced into it by other people's decisions, by other people's strategies. Those kind of limitations reduced the Executioner's effectiveness. He was, first and foremost, an offensive player. He took the fight to his enemies and knocked the fight out of them. He didn't wait for them to attack. His unique ability to infiltrate and disable, to wreak havoc inside the guard of a foe, proved over countless campaigns, had brought horror and death to mobsters, terrorists and drug kingpins alike.

He was a hot wind that scorched, and moved on.

This night he blew over Plantation Cay.

Kurtzman and the Stony Man team had pinpointed the estate as a highly probable hideout for del Borgo; it was certainly one of his possessions. They had worked backward from the Justice Department's list of possibles, tracing the histories of the current owners, their financial records, their blood and marriage ties.

What they had learned was that ten years earlier Rupert

Mahoney was a nobody, a sailing bum who made rent money by skippering other people's yachts from one coast to the other. Then, Mahoney's younger brother, Ronald, had married a Colombian national. She was the daughter of an army general with suspected Medellín drug connections. Shortly after his brother's wife had entered the U.S., things began to look up for Rupert. Suddenly he had a hefty bank account. Then he began to invest in real estate. He was very successful at it, or so it seemed. The sale of properties was his only apparent source of income.

DEA had gotten a warrant to search his premises just once. They had turned up nothing. But the flak they got from Mahoney's team of lawyers made them think twice about ever doing it again. Besides, it was obvious that Mahoney had nothing directly to do with the sale of cocaine in the U.S. His job was to launder del Borgo's drug money by spreading it all over Florida.

DEA and Justice surveillance, both aerial and electronic, of the Plantation Cay estate over the past week had indicated that the place had been invaded by several dozen South American gangsters. Some had been identified through recon photos as former button men for the cartel in the States; others were hired guns imported from Colombia. It was clear that the estate had been a staging area for the attacks on the members of R.

For that reason alone, it was due for demolition.

After clearing the water from inside his face mask, Bolan bit down on the snorkel's rubber mouthpiece and swam closer to the estate's broad wooden pier. He stopped forty yards from the end of the dock, well outside the halo cast by its floodlights, and took stock of what lay ahead of him.

A small wooden building stood on the water end of the pier. The structure's door was open, and outside it, two Colombian soldiers sat in chairs, smoking. The aroma of their cigars drifted down to Bolan, as did music from the party going on in the mansion.

Tied to the pier on Bolan's right were two Bertram sportfishing boats. The thirty-two-foot cabin cruisers were moored to a floating dock with their bows pointing toward the bay. On the other side of the pier, secured to a similar dock, was a forty-foot sailing sloop. The sportfishers were dark, but bright lights shone from inside the sailboat.

The Executioner could also see lights blazing from the rear of the mansion. It was possible that the El Salvadoran snipers were set up there. Using night-vision scopes, they could control the ground leading up the house.

There were only three of them now. The body of one sniper had been found during a postfirefight sweep of the mountains above the lake. Because of the massive destruction to the head and face, Bolan couldn't say positively that the corpse belonged to one of the men he had observed in action two years earlier. Formal identification had to be made through fingerprints. A search of El Salvadoran military records had been requested, but the results hadn't come back yet. Maybe they never would. Bolan thought it likely that all the snipers' records had vanished in 1993, the moment they left for Colombia.

The Executioner took a breath and dived, hardly making a ripple in the black surface. He swam underwater to the pilings at the end of the pier. Keeping to the shadows, he worked his way along the pilings to the stern of the first sportfisher. Treading water out of sight of the men on the pier and the mansion, he opened the waterproof bag he carried and removed a pair of HE limpet mines. He slipped back underwater and planted a suction mine on the keel of the first vessel, then repeated the procedure on the second. He came up for air between the two boats, then silently dogpaddled between the pilings to the other side of the pier.

There was coarse laughter inside the sloop. Bolan floated

in the darkness behind the gangway leading up to the pier and listened—three men, maybe four, he guessed. From their conversation, and mood, they were getting high on drugs. The soldiers had to sneak away from the house for this kind of recreation, as narcotics of any kind were strictly forbidden on the estate.

The Executioner swam the length of the sailboat underwater, pausing to plant two mines, one fore, one aft. In the waterproof bag he towed was the remote detonator for all four limpets.

Nobody was going to escape the estate by water, unless they swam.

Bolan dogpaddled back through the pilings to the gangway on the other side. Climbing up on the floating dock, he shed his dive gear and emptied the dry bag. Over his wet T-shirt and shorts, he donned a combat harness loaded with extra magazines for the Beretta, with flash, CS and frag grenades, and prerigged HE charges of C-4 plastique. He threaded the 93-R's sound suppressor onto its barrel and pulled a night-observation device over his head and down around his neck, out of the way until he needed it.

At the top of the gangway's steps, Bolan paused to make sure no one was approaching from the mansion. At the other end of the pier, about forty-five yards away, the two Colombians sat with their backs to him, watching the lights of Miami in the distance. He soundlessly crossed to the back side of the pier's guardhouse, the 93-R up and ready to eliminate the Colombians if they caught a glimpse of his movements.

Kneeling on the opposite side of the little house, the Executioner heard their breathing and smelled the smoke of their cigars and the heavy, sweet scent of their aftershave. They spoke in Spanish, discussing an upcoming trip with their boss, Rupert Mahoney, to Zurich—presumably for some kind of an illegal money transfer. A city of shoe clerks, one of them complained bitterly.

The bagman's bodyguard didn't have to worry about being bored to tears in Switzerland ever again.

Bolan looked back at the mansion, awaiting Hawkins's signal.

THE SECURITY MAN on the Mahoney estate front gate paused in midsip, lowering his half-quart, plastic coffee mug. A cockroach the size of a cigar butt had crept over the threshold of the guardhouse. The insect stood there, its antennae waving as it tasted the air.

It was a big one, fully two inches across the back and five inches long, a possible world record. Making no sudden or jerky moves, the security man set down his mug and reached across the desk for the rubber-band gun.

The contest had developed between the night-shift watchmen to see who could pot the most and biggest roaches. The winner claimed a weekly jackpot. It was symptomatic of the dullness of the job. There hadn't been any action at the Mahoney mansion since the DEA raid two years earlier. Given the isolation of the island site, and the elaborate security precautions, who in his right mind would try to rip off a Plantation Cay estate? And even if you were stupid enough to try, the last place you'd pick would be the mansion belonging to a Colombian drug lord.

The guards had started out with heavier anticockroach weaponry, pellet guns and the like, but solid hits tended to tear the bodies apart, which made for arguments over which pile of parts represented the bigger bug. The rubber-band gun temporarily incapacitated the quarry, which was then dropped into a lidded jar for later comparison.

Using his forearm for a gun rest, the security man fired. The roach took a full broadside hit and was sent skittering back out the door. It left behind several broken, mahogany-colored legs.

"Gotcha!" the guard said.

He picked up his specimen jar and stepped outside the kiosk to claim his weakly kicking prize. As he bent down to pick up the stunned insect, something coughed on the other side of the steel security gate.

He never heard it.

A subsonic 9 mm hollowpoint slug cored through the middle of his brain, pelting the broad-leaf bushes with gobbets of gray jelly and shards of skull. The guard crumpled noiselessly on the driveway.

Clad in a uniform and cap identical to the security man's, wearing a loaded day pack over one shoulder and a coil of aircraft cable over the other, T. J. Hawkins easily and quickly climbed the twelve-foot-high steel gate. As he cleared the top of the gate, he glanced at the video surveillance camera that surmounted the left-hand gatepost. It was motorized and on automatic scan. Hawkins hit the ground with thirty seconds left until the camera swung back on the gatehouse, thirty seconds until it revealed him to the main security-control center inside the mansion.

He secured the gate to the steel-reinforced concrete post with two wraps of quarter-inch, multistrand stainless-steel cable and a massive case-hardened padlock. As he turned away from the gate, the numbers had dropped to fifteen seconds. It was going to be close. He grabbed the dead security man by the armpits and, with a mighty heave, dumped him out of sight behind the kiosk. As the camera swept over Hawkins, he had the huge coffee mug up front of his face, blocking its view of his features.

After the camera moved on, he pulled the dead guard into the hut and set him up in the chair. He put the man's back to the lens and set his uniform bill cap far back on his head to hide the cavernous hole there.

Beyond the range of the camera, Hawkins stripped out of the gray-on-black security uniform, revealing the combat blacksuit beneath. From the day pack he pulled out a fully packed battle harness. After checking his 93-R, he resumed the hunt.

He had seen two other men, not in uniform, patrolling the front of the estate. He moved cautiously forward along the shadowy edge of the driveway that twisted through the estate's front gardens, the silenced Beretta in autofire mode and ready to rip.

A Colombian soldier unexpectedly stepped from the foliage not ten feet in front of him.

The surprise was mutual, and life suddenly hinged on the outcome of a quick-draw contest.

The gunman's machine pistol hung at his side, suspended over his shoulder on a black ballistic nylon strap. Before he could shoot, he had to get hold of the mini-Uzi's grip, depress the grip safety, thumb off the trigger safety and aim.

So it was really no contest at all.

Hawkins's 93-R triple-timed into the front of the Colombian's throat, and the man toppled sideways into the flower beds. When he picked up the mini-Uzi, Hawkins saw the select-fire indicator was still on S. He slung the weapon over his shoulder and dragged the man by the heels deep into the dense shrubbery.

"Rómulo?" a voice said from the driveway.

Hawkins dropped to one knee.

"Where are you, Rómulo?"

The sports-jacket-clad soldier looked right at Hawkins and the dead man without seeing them. Then he walked on, again calling softly to his patrol partner.

Hawkins stepped out from the bush, raised the Beretta and fired once from a distance of less than five feet into the base of the man's skull. The force of the bullet's impact sent the Colombian crashing down onto what little was left of his face.

After hauling the body into the bushes, Hawkins made his way toward the mansion. He kept to the shadows along the driveway until he was directly across the redbrick parking apron from the front entry. Two stretch limousines and a Ford Explorer were parked in front of the house. Hawkins removed three small parcels of C-4 from his harness. He armed their remote detonators, then deftly shuffleboarded them over the smooth driveway, skidding them under the bodies of the cars.

Thanks to the loud salsa music coming from inside the mansion, the four plainclothes guards at the front door didn't hear or see a thing. They seemed much more interested in talking to one another than in watching over the parked vehicles.

Hawkins found the brick path around the side of the mansion and followed it. He stopped when he came across a suitably dark, sub-ground-floor window. He hopped down into the window's light well and took a glass cutter from his vest. He was betting that the laser and infrared alarms and the vibration sensors wouldn't be activated this early in the evening, not with a party going on and a houseful of armed men to provide protection.

He cut a circular hole in the window and reached through to undo the latch. Raising the window, he crawled through and dropped silently to the floor inside. From his pack he removed a night-vision device and put it on. There was no need to refer to a map: he had memorized the mansion's floor plan. Hawkins slipped quickly through the eerie green world, trying door handles, clearing the basement rooms. He didn't want somebody coming up on him from behind. If a door was locked, he figured nobody was at home and moved on. When he came across the door with the hasp and an unlocked lock stuck in it, he didn't even bother to try it.

Hawkins found the main power box in a far corner of the basement. Beside it was the mansion's emergency backup, gas-powered generator. He disconnected the backup's starter motor, then popped the lid on the power box and located the main breakers. As planned, he blacked out the mansion for one second, then returned the power.

He waited, eyes focused on the phosphorescent sweep hand of his dive watch, his finger on the breakers' trip lever. In another two minutes, the lights would go out on the Mahoney estate.

For good.

13

When the lights winked out in the mansion, the entire estate, including the guardhouse on the end of the pier and the sailboat tied up to it, went dark, too. Power returned almost instantly.

"What was that?" one of the men guarding the pier said.

"Nothing," the other soldier replied.

On the opposite side of the guardhouse, Mack Bolan crouched and waited for the numbers to fall. When one minute and fifty seconds had passed after the lights came back on, he fitted the AN/PVS-7 night-vision device to his face and, closing his shooting eye, switched it on. Shades of painfully bright, luminous green defined Bolan's reality.

At an elapsed time of two minutes everything went dark again, for everyone but Bolan and Hawkins. It was their way of evening the long odds against them.

"Damn," the guard said as once again, temporary blindness struck him.

Bolan was already rounding the side of the guardhouse.

One subsonic round from the 93-R took out guard number one.

The second drug soldier recognized the sound of a suppressed gunshot and felt the splash of warm gore across his cheek as his companion's head went to pieces. Before the man could raise his machine pistol, Bolan shot him in the temple.

The close-range bullet wounds were devastating, and

there was no need to check the bodies for signs of life. The Executioner turned and headed for the mansion, the detonator in his left hand, the Beretta in his right.

As he sprinted over the pier's decking, a bright beam of light struck him. Instinctively he shut his shooting eye and kept running. The spotlight came from below, from the foredeck of the sloop, pinning him like an actor on a stage.

The sight of an armed man running full speed, night-vision goggles on his head, drew an immediate reaction from the soldiers on the sailboat. Autofire chattered up at him, gnawing the pier's railing, gouging chunks out of its deck. They had a bad angle on a very rapidly moving target.

Without turning his head or breaking stride, Bolan swung the Beretta's barrel over the railing, spraying the sloop's front deck with tribursts of 9 mm slugs. The searchlight suddenly veered away from him, then speared straight up into space, a phosphorescent green column.

Over the sound of his own footfalls and breathing Bolan could hear the men on the sloop scrambling for the floating dock and the pier's gangway. They made him press the detonator's fire switch sooner than he would have liked. As he did so, he shut his eyes tight.

Behind him fireballs of orange blossomed on both sides of the pier. The sportfishers and the sloop disintegrated, their hulls and superstructures hurtling in all directions; the explosion tore apart the men on the dock, and the shock wave of the blast made Bolan stumble. He recovered his balance, catlike, in midair and, opening his eyes, continued to race toward the rear of the mansion, which was more than a hundred yards away.

Before he reached it, the building was suddenly backlit as a horrendous concussion rocked its front side. Bolan again instinctively looked away to avoid the blinding flare of green that leaped high into the night sky.

Hawkins had crashed the party.

THE COLOMBIANS standing watch at the rear of the house blinked in the darkness. Then the sounds and flash of gunfire erupted from the sailboat tied up to the pier. Even as they brought their weapons to bear, the pier exploded in a colossal billow of orange before their eyes. For a second, against the glare of the synchronized detonations, they saw a running man. They blinked again and he was gone.

A roar shook the ground under their feet and blew out every window in the mansion's first floor. Plate-glass needles whooshed across the flagstones at their feet.

Realizing they were under full-out attack, the guards quickly ducked to cover behind the life-size statuary and heavy stone railings that led up to the rear courtyard.

One of them, overeager to join with the unseen enemy, opened fire on nothing.

They all joined in, spraying the slope leading down to the pier with unaimed 9 mm lead.

BOLAN OPENED HIS EYES in time to see green figures disperse over the courtyard's stairs. He cut a sharp right turn from the main path, pouring on the speed. When they began to search the grounds with fire, he was already on their flank, well out of the kill zone. At the corner of the building, he scrambled over the stone railing and onto the raised courtyard. If he made any noise, it was masked by the canvas-ripping sound of full-auto bursts.

"Stop shooting!" one of the Colombians shouted.

When they did, they heard gunfire erupt from deep inside the house.

A second's pause. A break in concentration as they listened. It was all the Executioner needed.

Bolan picked his way around the lawn chairs and statues, then raced along the back side of the house. Switching the

Beretta to his left hand, he charged into the faces of the first two Colombians in front of him and shot them both in the head. As he'd known they would, the muzzle-flashes gave him away. One of the soldiers brought up his Uzi, firing in panic before he had acquired a target. Bullets sparked on the flagstones between his feet as Bolan triple-thumped him with 115-grain hollowpoint rounds to the center of his chest.

The last man had seen enough. He deserted his post, racing for the stone balustrade that marked the courtyard's perimeter and the deeper darkness of the gardens beyond. Bolan unleashed another 3-shot burst, chopping him down before he reached the railing.

As the Executioner edged open the mansion's rear door, screams and gunshots erupted from within. Dropping to his stomach, he poked his head around the bottom of the door. A cluster of phosphor-green figures jockeyed for shooting positions in the arches and doorways of the hall. He ducked back as random, searching fire swept out the entryway.

RUPERT MAHONEY DIDN'T think much about it when the lights flickered out the first time. Such things happened occasionally on the Cay when a storm brought down a power line. Sometimes the power went out completely, and for days, which was why he had had an emergency-power system installed.

When the lights went out the second time, and the power didn't immediately kick back in, Mahoney had a premonition of impending disaster. When gunfire crackled from the rear of the grounds, confirming his fears, the short hairs on the back of his neck sprang to full attention. From the window of the ballroom, he saw the enormous flash as the three boats exploded, taking half the pier with them.

It had just registered in his brain that they were under attack when the front of the building quaked, sheets of glass crashing out of their frames, priceless works of art toppling from their pedestals.

In darkness, surrounded by jostling, cursing men, Mahoney tried to figure out what was going on and who was behind it. It wasn't DEA. DEA had learned its lesson with the barrage of harassment-and-damage suits he had initiated; they were still fighting the loops of legal tanglewire he had set in place. This was a military-style all-out assault, not a police action. No one had asked for a surrender; no one was going to. It wasn't the Justice Department, either.

He doubted that the Cali cartel would pull a trick like this. Bombs and bullets weren't their usual style, and besides, what did they have to fight about? They had already won the cocaine turf war.

Whoever it was appeared to be advancing in force and they were taking no prisoners. They had to have overrun the security teams at the front gate and the pier. Automatic fire rattled from the rear of the house and the kitchen. It dawned on Mahoney then that the enemy was already inside the house, choosing to fight in darkness. Which meant they had to have night-vision devices, something most police departments didn't possess.

Who were these guys?

Mahoney's own forces were scattered through the big house. Some of the soldiers who had taken women to the upstairs bedrooms hadn't returned. He tried to recall how many were still in the ballroom with him. Eight? Ten? It was hard to think with all the racket going on.

"Shut up!" he bellowed into the darkness.

The noise stopped.

"Get something in front of the doors to the corridor," he ordered the Colombians. "Pile up those couches and chairs. Make a barricade."

The faint light coming from the burning pier and cars allowed him to see the outline of his soldiers manhandling the furniture. They needed to set up some kind of defensive position inside the ballroom: the barricade wouldn't hold for long. They could've held the whores for hostages, maybe even bargained for their lives, but they were all upstairs.

"Drag those tables to the foot of the stage," he told the Colombians. "Tip them over."

Mahoney knew that any defense they came up with was going to be futile. They didn't have the ammunition or manpower to hold out for long and their opponents weren't going to accept any white flags. He was already thinking through his own, private escape plan, which required that everyone else stay there and die.

HAWKINS DIVED behind the stainless-steel counter as a flurry of autofire clanged, then dropped the hanging pots and pans. Beside the counter, almost underneath him, a small man in a white chef's hat and uniform lay trembling, his hands behind his head, fingers interlaced.

"Don't kill me," the chef said.

"How many kitchen helpers are in here?" Hawkins demanded.

"Just me and two others."

"Where are they?"

"They hid in the freezer. I couldn't get to it."

"Shh," Hawkins warned him. He heard footsteps on the other side of the kitchen. The Colombians were moving, trying to get an angle on him in the dark. He unclipped a stun grenade from his vest. "Stay flat on the floor and you'll be okay," he told the chef, then tossed the grenade over the counter.

An instant before the grenade detonated, he covered the lens of the AN/PVS-7 with his hand. If he hadn't, the intensity of the flash would've blinded him for hours. The concussion knocked all the remaining cookware off the overhead racks.

It was still clattering as he stood, searching for targets.

A man in a security uniform staggered backward, his hand to his face. Hawkins shot him through the heart, and the man groaned in agony as he dropped to the floor.

Two more dazed security men stumbled around on the opposite side of the kitchen, their weapons lowered. Hawkins swept them with a series of tribursts, spinning them and sending them crashing into the wall.

As he moved to the kitchen's far door, Hawkins dropped the Beretta's empty magazine and quickly slapped a full one home.

BOLAN ROLLED a stun grenade into the rear hallway. The moment it roared, he rounded the doorway and waded into the bedlam of battle. The blinded, deafened Colombians knew he was coming, and they were momentarily powerless to do anything about it. A pair of soldiers hiding in rooms opposite along the corridor opened fire. Terrified and disoriented, they swept not Bolan, but each other with point-blank autofire, blasting each other back into the rooms, out of sight.

The Executioner shot another man out of a doorway with a single bullet to the throat. As he stepped over the thrashing gunman, he checked his face. It wasn't del Borgo.

He unclipped another stunner from his harness and tossed it around a right-hand corner of the hall, into the sunken rear living room. The grenade hit the back of the U-shaped array of leather couches and bounced onto the cushions, detonating within a foot of the Colombian soldier hiding there.

Bolan turned the corner with the Beretta leading the way. The gunner lay on his back on the polar bear rug.

It wasn't del Borgo.

Before Bolan could straighten, bullets crashed into the fireplace's marble mantel, missing him by inches. As the Executioner half turned, he saw two figures disappear behind a doorway farther down the corridor. He pulled a frag grenade from his vest and lobbed it through the open doorway.

The house quaked from the explosion. When Bolan looked around the blackened, smoking door frame, he saw not two, but three bodies sprawled on the floor. He turned them over, checking their features against a face he had burned into his memory.

No del Borgo.

Ahead the hallway ended in a huge foyer, which was part of the mansion's main entrance. Bolan moved quickly to the hall's last archway, checking the anteroom for targets. At the foot of the wide staircase, a man with a gun ducked for cover.

The Executioner didn't shoot. The man was wearing a night-vision device.

Hawkins silently crossed the pink marble floor and joined him inside the archway.

"First floor is all clear on my side," Hawkins said. "Yours, too?"

Bolan nodded. "All we have left down here is the ballroom," he stated, indicating the set of doors in the foyer wall to their left. "I imagine we've trapped a lot of them in there. Let's get the doors down and see."

While Hawkins covered the ballroom's entrance, he knelt and started removing C-4 parcels from his combat vest. When he was all set, Bolan moved to the doors and placed an HE charge on each. As he finished with the last, a hail of gunfire ripped through the door and the adjoining wall. Under the flying splinters and plaster, Bolan tucked and rolled away, coming up on his feet, weapon in hand.

14

Tacho Ruiz awoke with a violent start as the storeroom's ceiling collapsed on top of him, chunks of plasterboard bouncing off his face and chest. He sat bolt upright on the mattress, his ears ringing from the boom of an explosion that had gone off almost directly overhead.

In the darkness and choking plaster dust, his first impulse was to reach out for Gaspar. Then he remembered his brother's cratered head, the unsocketed eyes dangling by their nerve bundles, the bisected neck vessels geysering blood as his still-living heart pumped out its last few beats.

Gaspar was gone.

Tacho screamed at the blackness, throwing the debris from his legs and jumping to his feet. He found the door handle. It turned, but the door wouldn't open. He threw himself against the inside of the door repeatedly.

He couldn't break it down.

Above him, in the corridors of the great house, gunfire raged back and forth. He was only dimly aware of it. Tacho was lost in a world of grief and heartbreak.

For a moment all the strength went out of him, and he sagged to the floor. How could he live without Gaspar, his other half? They had shared something that much deeper than simple blood ties. They lusted the same lust. They saw themselves reflected in each other's eyes.

Tacho even owed his crocodile teeth to his brother. Gaspar had knocked them into dagger points with a ball-peen hammer when they were fifteen. He had done it at Tacho's request, Tacho who had needed to find his own limits of pain and machismo, who had needed to show the world every time he smiled that he had no such limits. They both had been proud of Tacho's jagged teeth, proud of the looks of awe and horror they brought.

As members of the Atlacatl Battalion, they had reinvented the world, made it a place of darkness and terror and reveled in it. They had made beasts of themselves and reveled in that, too. The blood of the conquistadores ran hot in their veins.

But the blue-eyed North American had stolen all that they had worked for. His bullet had plundered Gaspar's skull and changed everything in a single instant. He had to pay, and pay horribly.

He had to answer to the beast.

Tacho's strength returned in a rush. His soul demanded something be destroyed. Anything. In a fury, he threw himself upon the mattress. He tore the striped canvas cover with his teeth, then with his bare hands, ripped it apart and began to disembowel the cottony insides with clawed fingers.

THE SOLDIER LISTENING in the darkness by the ballroom's front doors heard something, a soft footfall on the other side, then another. He dived out of the way and when he was clear, he whistled once. Across the ballroom, the nine other Colombians standing behind Mahoney's tabletop defensive wall opened fire. In the strobe light of muzzle-flashes, Mahoney could see the doors and wall pocked by their barrage of bullets.

A second later the room was rocked by a terrible explosion and, as if punched by a gigantic fist, the heavy oak doors flew inward off their hinges, spinning and crashing onto the ballroom floor.

The Colombians swept the black, smoke-filled entryway with a hail of 9 mm slugs.

Mahoney knew it wouldn't do any good.

"Keep shooting!" he said, encouraging his men even as he stepped back from the firing line and moved toward the nearest, glassless window frame.

MACK BOLAN TURNED his back to the doorway and, covering his head, tripped the detonator's firing switch. The force of the blast hurled him down hard on both knees. Shaking off the impact, he looked across the foyer to Hawkins, who reappeared from behind the hallway arch.

Bullets whined through the air as the Colombians in the ballroom tried to forestall a frontal assault. The Executioner had moved too far forward to take the battle to the next level; he no longer had a wide enough angle on the doorway. Hawkins, on the other hand, was out of the drug soldiers' line of fire and still had a clear shot into the ballroom.

Bolan stripped out of his combat vest, removed three magazines and stuffed them into the pocket of his shorts. Then he slid the vest across the marble floor to Hawkins.

Hawkins quickly stripped the vest of its fragmentation grenades. After removing the remaining frags from his own harness, he pulled the pin on one and lobbed the bomb into the ballroom. It bounced out of sight around the corner of the doorway.

He ducked back behind the wall, waiting for the explosion.

The racking blast was followed by screams and a pall of corrosive smoke that billowed out of the doorway.

Hawkins tossed in two more grenades, banking them off the ballroom wall and into the middle of the room.

After the third one exploded, he had to pull the night-vision goggles off his face. A raging fire had started inside the ballroom, its dancing light hurting his eyes. He noticed that Bolan had also removed his goggles. Hawkins could feel the fire's heat from sixty feet away.

When the fourth grenade went off, there were no answering screams, but the ballroom's sprinkler system kicked in. Water sprayed down on them from jets concealed in the ceiling.

Hawkins held up a last grenade in the flickering light.

The Executioner nodded and prepared to charge the ballroom.

When the grenade whumped inside the room, Bolan and Hawkins burst through the ruined doorway.

Despite the hissing sprinklers, half the room was on fire. The other half was ripped by shrapnel and stained with smoke. It stank of spent explosive, burning furniture and ruptured humanity. The tabletop barricade in front of the stage had been blown apart by the successive grenade blasts. The men who had taken cover behind it lay like rags in a bloody heap.

Up on the ballroom's stage, a gun muzzle poked out from behind the back curtain.

Bolan and Hawkins saw him at the same instant. They fired simultaneously, sending double tribursts of lead thwacking into the curtain, dropping the drug soldier before he got off a round. As the nameless, faceless, would-be assassin thudded to the floor behind the heavy drapery, the soles of his shoes popped out from under its bottom edge.

Another form ruffled the curtain from the back side, moving away from the body.

Again the two warriors fired in unison.

The curtain puffed dust as hollowpoint slugs slammed it and the torso of the fleeing man behind it. The Colombian had to have bounced off something backstage, pulley ropes, a sound-system speaker, because when hit by their multiple-round bursts, he sprawled toward them and as he did so, the bottom of the curtain lifted. The man's head and shoulders emerged from under the curtain as he fell forward onto the stage.

Bolan put his combat vest back on, and they set about turning over the newly dead, looking for a face that wasn't there. They worked quickly, and when they were done, they returned to the foyer and the staircase leading to the second floor.

RUPERT MAHONEY WAS halfway out the window frame when the first grenade went off, the explosion blowing him out of the building. He landed hard on the flower beds outside. Even as he bounced on the ground, he knew he had been hit by a fragment of the grenade. The back of his right thigh burned with pain.

It didn't keep him from getting up and running, though. More grenades whumped inside the ballroom, their detonations momentarily drowning out the screams of the Colombians.

He knew he only had one chance to survive, and that was to make it to the water.

The burning mansion lit his way down the path to the ruined pier. At every stride he expected to be shot by a marksman waiting in the bushes.

When he finally dashed across the white sand beach and slipped into the black water, he felt an enormous sense of relief. He'd never had quite that close a brush with death before.

He dived underwater and kicked off his shoes, then stroked off at an angle to the pier. He surfaced for air, barely raising his nostrils above the water. In the distance the mansion fires were dimming. Mahoney was glad it wasn't really his house. Facing del Borgo with the bad news wasn't going to be fun. The Colombian had been counting on the cash to pay off his immediate debts and slip deeper into obscurity. But first things first.

He started a measured Australian crawl, slow and quiet, heading for the point of land that separated the estate from its nearest neighbor. Mahoney swam five times that far for recreation on a daily basis. For that reason, he figured he was home free. Up to this point, he had led a charmed life. Things just fell into his lap. When the shit hit the fan, it always missed him and splattered the guy beside him.

About halfway to the point, he noticed a sharp twinge in the back of his thigh where he had been wounded. It throbbed every time he kicked that leg, but the pain didn't get any worse, and he kept on swimming.

A few minutes later he began to feel an unusual fatigue. This alarmed him because he shouldn't have been tired that soon. The sense of weakness increased with every stroke, until he could barely lift his arms.

Bobbing, three hundred yards from shore, from safety, from a continuation of the good life, Rupert Mahoney realized he wasn't going to make it. The exertion of swimming had caused the shrapnel in his thigh to cut deeper; it had severed a vein. In the warm water, he was rapidly bleeding to death. He looked up at the starless sky and steeled himself for a final judgment that he knew would be harsh indeed.

ON LEGS OF RUBBER, on knees that trembled uncontrollably, Deborah Ailes allowed herself to be led, through the dark bedroom into the darker bathroom. She recalled that for a few moments, down in the ballroom, after the effects of the vodka martinis she'd gulped began to kick in, she'd been able to tell herself that she was a big girl, that she could handle anything and that whatever happened, it was worth it to get the money.

She'd been wrong.

Ashley Rossignol pulled her deeper into the bathroom. They both were in their underwear. The two women had formed a new interpersonal bond that night. They had been laid out side by side on the queen-size bed before the Colombians started to take turns. The men had urged one another on; it was some kind of a contest.

Rossignol had her hand out in front of her, feeling for something along the wall. Her fingers found a handle, and an unseen panel opened out and down—the laundry chute.

The room quaked from an explosion downstairs, making them clutch at the wall for support.

Ailes didn't object as her companion helped her to step into the narrow chute. Ordinarily the darkness and the pressure of metal all around her would've brought on an attack of claustrophobia, but she was numbed to the core, her mind and body separated as if by surgery. She dropped down the aluminum shaft, the metal squealing on her bare skin. Then it was gone and she was in free-fall, dropping into a pile of damp bedclothes.

The real-estate broker fell down beside her.

"Are you okay?" the broker whispered.

As long as the men were gone, as long as the ordeal was over, nothing else mattered.

"We can't stay here," Rossignol told her. "We've got to find someplace to hide until the police arrive."

Ailes allowed herself to be pulled to her feet. Rossignol found the door to the laundry room, and they slipped out into the basement hall. Above them, more explosions went off, one after another. They could hear the screams of the wounded through the ceiling.

People were being killed up there, Ailes thought, people who deserved to die.

Her companion dragged her along the hallway, trying the doors, looking for a place where they wouldn't be discovered.

About halfway down the corridor, her fingers touched a door with a hasp screwed into its frame. There was a padlock stuck through it, holding the door closed. When Rossignol grabbed the lock, it turned under her fingers. It wasn't clicked shut.

"This might be the place," she told Ailes. "No one is going to look for us in here."

Rossignol lifted the lock from the hasp and pushed the door open a crack. It was too dark for her to see anything inside. There weren't even any windows to let the firelight in.

It seemed safe to her.

She entered the room and pulled Ailes in behind her, then she closed the door. As the broker moved to the center of the room, her bare toe stubbed on some rubble on the floor.

"Ow," she said softly, hopping on the other foot.

"Shh," Ailes said, squeezing her hand.

"What?"

Ailes didn't answer.

"What is it?" she repeated, giving the woman's arm a hard shake.

"Can't you hear it?" Ailes asked. Her voice was thin and reedy with terror.

"Hear what?"

"Listen."

"I don't hear anything."

"Stop breathing for a second."

Rossignol held her breath, and that's when she heard it, over the pounding of her own heart.

The sound of someone else breathing. They weren't alone.

15

Barbara Price put her hands in the air, asking for a moment of calm. "Come on, you, two," she said, "I know you're tired. We're all tired. But don't take it out on each other. You're arguing over how many angels can dance on the head of a pin. It isn't relevant to what's on our plate."

Akira Tokaido pulled himself together. He took a breath and let it out very slowly. He nodded to the mission controller, then turned to the red-haired woman at the computer terminal next to his. "I'm sorry," he said. "I shouldn't have said what I did."

Carmen Delahunt wasn't quite ready to call a truce. "If you'd been right, I wouldn't have minded, but you weren't right."

"Okay, Carmen," Price said with finality, "that's enough."

"Right," the redhead conceded.

Price looked at Kurtzman. Around his eyes and the corners of his mouth, he was showing the strain of the long, tension-filled night, and the prospect of more to come. They had risked the lives of two of the best fighting men she had ever known by sending them in against enormous odds, and now it looked like they were going to have to do it all over again.

Scattered over Kurtzman's U-shaped desk were printouts and diagrams, satellite and aerial-recon photos of a Thoroughbred horse farm. The one-thousand-acre estate was set in the rolling-hill country outside Ocala, Florida. It was best guess number two as to the current whereabouts of Raffi del Borgo, former Medellín cartel underlord, current fugitive from justice.

The recon photos taken the previous morning showed a man resembling del Borgo moving between the main house and the stable. When blown up, the aerial shots had proved too grainy for a positive ID by Justice. Using a new computerized image-enhancement program that Hunt Wethers was developing, the Stony Man team had managed to improve the picture enough for a ninety percent positive ID on del Borgo.

It then remained to fill in some of the gaps in the facts, which was what half the Stony Man team had been working on since before daybreak.

The forty-million-dollar Thoroughbred farm was owned and operated by a former Miami vice detective. According to official police sources, some five years ago Peter "Bud" Hylander had inherited a vast sum of money from a long-lost relative. The inheritance allowed him to retire early from the force. At the time of his departure, rumors were starting to circulate about his connection with the Colombian cartel—specifically that he was on its payroll. Hylander had left before any formal investigation could be made. Subsequent, highly discreet inquiries by the FBI had failed to find any direct link between Hylander and the Medellín cartel.

According to tax records, the stud farm had operated at a substantial profit for the past two years. Hylander was a successful local businessman, and a former cop with an unblemished service record. Justice had decided to tread lightly upon his well-manicured toes.

The maps and charts on Kurtzman's desk showed the distances between and elevations of the low hills surrounding the estate's main building complex. The Stony Man team also had acquired a set of architect's plans for the sprawling, split-level house.

It was amazing what you could shake out with a federal warrant at three in the morning, Price thought.

The last Justice fly-by had been at 7:00 p.m. the previous evening. Nothing unusual was recorded by the recon camera, no evidence of an influx of nonfarm personnel, no sign of the principal actors that they sought.

Around midnight, ground surveillance noted a helicopter landing near the estate's pond. About a half-dozen people got out and crossed to the main building. This arrival time coincided with reports from Bolan and Hawkins of a departing chopper moments before the attack on the Cay began. The helicopter was still parked at the horse farm in the morning.

Unlike the Plantation Cay property, the horse farm wasn't a defensive stronghold. There was no water perimeter. There wasn't even a secure fence; the property was bounded by split rail and wire. The question the Stony Man team had to ask was, given its limitations, why had del Borgo chosen that place to go to ground?

Wethers thought it was desperation, pure and simple. If del Borgo needed cash fast, he would try to sell his most marketable property first. Undoubtedly that was Plantation Cay. Del Borgo wouldn't want to hole up there if he anticipated a quick sale. Carmen Delahunt had suggested that because the trail connecting the Thoroughbred farm to him was hazier, the drug lord might think it less likely to be discovered as part of his U.S. holdings.

Either scenario was plausible.

"How much longer until they have all the material in hand?" Hal Brognola asked. He was the only one in the computer lab who looked fresh that morning. The quarts of coffee he'd gulped the previous night had held off the exhaustion brought on by his head injury for only so long.

He had fallen asleep in his wheelchair at around 2:00 a.m. They'd covered him with a blanket, and he'd slept peacefully through the rest of the night.

Kurtzman checked the numbers scrolling on his monitor. "Another two minutes and we'll be ready to talk to them."

"Are you going to tell them about the basement?" Tokaido asked, picking up a photo from Kurtzman's deck and staring at it. When he looked up from the single page, his expression showed both anger and revulsion.

"I haven't decided, yet," Brognola replied. "We don't really know if or how it's connected to this operation. For all we know, the perpetrator may be among the unidentified dead at the Cay."

"Well, here's hoping," Delahunt said, showing Price her crossed fingers.

"We aren't going to have solid answers from the crime scene for many hours yet," Brognola went on. "The call girls who survived the assault haven't been much help. They're either too scared to talk or they really don't know anything about it."

"So all we can do is assume the bastard's still around and follow his instructions," Price said, glancing up at the bank of TV sets. They were tuned to various stations, national and local. The sound was set on scan mode, switching from station to station every five seconds, and was linked into the computer system. The computer had been programmed to respond to certain words—*murder, killer, victim*—by immediately increasing the volume to an audible level. That way, they didn't have to waste time monitoring the total output of news and weather.

"We're through sending data now," Kurtzman said. "We'll give them another minute to catch up on the hard copy, then we'll teleconference."

BOLAN CLOSED THE CURTAIN on the deserted parking lot. The Surf and Sand Motel was nowhere near sea or beach, but it was close enough to Miami International Airport for the walls to vibrate every time a passenger jet dropped in for a landing, which was every couple of minutes.

The Executioner turned back to the motel room's twin beds, where Grimaldi and Hawkins sat. Sheets of computer paper were spread out over the quilted coverlets and spilled onto the stained carpet.

The laptop computer, which was now acting as a phone, rang and then automatically made the scramble-connection to Stony Man Farm.

"This is the Bear," a voice said.

Hawkins boosted the gain until the speaker crackled, then backed off the volume a bit.

"Read you loud and clear," he said into the computer's built-in mike, which functioned as a speakerphone.

"Same here. Any questions about the material you received?"

"The numbers of opposition on-site," Bolan said. "Your estimates are vague."

"I know," Kurtzman said. "Sorry about that. We just don't have any hard data. No visuals. Water is on a well system, so we can't judge by that. Power use is well above the normal range for the time of year. That's indirect evidence, but it isn't conclusive, of course. We know about how many men he's used in the attacks so far, and how many are dead at the Cay. That doesn't mean he's shown us all he's got."

"Bottom line," Price cut in, "is to watch yourselves. Del Borgo could have an army hidden there."

"We don't necessarily have to confront them to accomplish the mission," Hawkins said.

"This is Hal here. Does that mean you've settled on an assault plan?"

"The two-hundred-foot-elevation hill, one thousand

yards out," Bolan said, "and the fifty-foot hill, three hundred yards out give us control of the main building and surrounding grounds. It's possible we can knock out del Borgo and the snipers at rifle distance. If that doesn't work, then we'll have no choice but to do a room-broom routine through the house and all the outbuildings."

"What's your ETA?" Brognola asked.

Grimaldi leaned toward the mike. "It's 260 miles to Ocala, Hal. That'll make it two hours plus from here to the target. Another hour to get into position. By midafternoon we'll be ready to rock."

"Is there anything else we need to know?" Hawkins asked.

There was a pause at the Stony Man end.

"No," Brognola said at last, "that's it for now."

"We'll contact you when we're ready to move into position," Hawkins said, and broke the connection.

Grimaldi started to pull together the vital paperwork: maps of the estate's grounds, with elevations, and the interior layout of its buildings. The stuff that had to be duplicated, he copied using the computer's printer. Meanwhile, Bolan outfitted his combat harness with frag grenades and full magazines for the 93-R. When he finished, he lifted a hard-shell gun case from the carpet and set it on the bed.

"What's that?" Hawkins asked, looking up from his own half-full battle vest.

Bolan lifted the thirty-six-pound scoped rifle from its padded case.

Hawkins recognized it immediately by its distinctive silhouette. It had a twenty-nine-inch free-floated fluted barrel, a solid built-in bipod and a Match-grade trigger. The cheek rest and buttstock were adjustable, and it had a harmonic balancer in the fore end to reduce barrel vibrations and improve shot groups. A muzzle brake helped tame the wicked recoil produced by the big cartridge it was designed around. "An AMAC .50!" he exclaimed. "All right!"

"A .50-cal sniper gun?" Grimaldi said, fascinated by the clamshell muzzle brake and the diameter of the gun's bore. "Damn, that thing's kick could probably break a shoulder."

"It would if you let it," Bolan said, opening the single shot bolt action. "This is what you reach out and touch somebody with at a thousand yards or better."

"And when you touch someone with one of these honeys," Hawkins said, picking up one of the machined-steel, 750-grain Dabco bullets from a box inside the case, "they don't *ever* forget it." The gun case also held a box of black-tipped, M-2 armor-piercing, 709-grain bullets, and another of 700-grain Dabco hollowpoint rounds.

"We used AMACs in Desert Storm," Hawkins told Grimaldi. "Nothing like a .50-caliber hole to screw up a Scud's guidance system." He looked at the weapon's scope with interest. "You can't be shooting at a thousand yards with a 16-power scope."

"No," Bolan replied, "I've got a 2-power converter on the Mk 4 Ultra. Brings it up to 32 power. I get some mirage, but that's to be expected. I've also got a custom cam for the BDC. It adjusts the scope internally out to three thousand yards."

"A Marine in Nam made a confirmed kill out to nearly that range with a .50," Grimaldi said.

"Yeah," Hawkins said, "I read a book about that. I've never used a .50 on a human being, only on Scuds and parked aircraft out to fifteen hundred to eighteen hundred yards. Before Saddam hid all his MiG-29 fighters, we used to take turns at that range trying to shoot out their front windscreens while they were sitting on the tarmac. Mind you, those windscreens aren't much bigger than a phone book. Once we blew one out, the plane was history, couldn't be flown for the three days it took the glue to dry after the mechanics had reset the glass. That meant we had three whole days to ventilate it with M-2 armor-piercing rounds.''

"Do you want to take the one-thousand-yard position?" Bolan asked.

"Sure. Thanks. I'd enjoy that."

The Executioner pointed out the spiral notebook tucked in a pocket inside the case. "The ballistic data on those three bullets is logged in the book, along with other performance information."

"I'll read it on the way," Hawkins replied.

HAL BROGNOLA DIDN'T HAVE to explain or defend his decision to withhold the FAX photo from Bolan. He'd already made it clear to Price, Kurtzman and the others that until more information came in, he considered the photo to be outside the framework of and extraneous to the current mission. Because he was their immediate superior, and because they fully trusted his judgment, that was enough.

The trouble was, the big Fed wanted the Executioner to see the photo ASAP.

In his heart of hearts, he had no doubt that it was connected to del Borgo in some way. But gut feeling wasn't proof. And he had an obligation to eliminate the unnecessary, to focus the attention of his people on getting things done, one at a time. If the Plantation Cay operation was anything to go by, Bolan, Hawkins and Grimaldi didn't need anything more to worry about.

Brognola looked down at the grainy, overexposed photo in his lap. It showed tall letters crudely painted on a basement wall, letters that he knew had been painted in still-warm human blood.

The note read Blue-Eyes, Watch The TV.

16

Renata Brush had told herself that if she was ever out driving in her car and someone suspicious approached her at a stoplight, before she'd let herself be carjacked and maybe murdered, she'd stomp the gas and speed away.

As often as she had rehearsed the scenario in her mind—the push of acceleration, the swerve as she maneuvered around other cars, light posts, bus-stop benches—when the time came to put up or shut up, she froze.

It all happened so quickly.

She didn't see the man cross the street. He came up on the car from behind. The shadow of his movement in the rearview mirror had caught her eye, but by the time she realized it was a person, he was already sliding up to the driver's door.

Even so, she might have roared away if she hadn't taken a second to look at him. She remembered the tension in her ankle as she prepared to lay rubber. Then he brought up the rifle from under the coat he was carrying. He pointed it at her head, and she froze like a jackrabbit caught in onrushing headlights.

He smiled at her, and at that instant, in some deep corner of her consciousness, she knew she was dead.

She drove now at the snaggletoothed man's direction. He sat in the back seat, with the end of the rifle barrel pushed between the front seats, angled into her right side. It looked like a hunting rifle—it had a telescopic sight—but it was all gray, like a military weapon.

"Are you a soldier?" she asked, attempting to make some kind of human contact with her kidnapper.

No answer.

He appeared to be Hispanic. *"¿Soldado? ¿Militar?"* she asked.

No answer.

"Why don't you just take my car and let me go?" Brush probed. "You don't have to hurt me."

The man pointed with his free hand. He wanted her to take a right turn off the two-lane highway and head toward an irrigation canal that ran between an expanse of cultivated fields.

Renata Brush could sense her time was running out.

"I have a daughter and grandchildren," she said desperately. *"Hija y nietos."*

No answer.

He made her drive along the canal a little way. The sky was getting light in the east. A new day was dawning, she thought, one that she probably wouldn't live to see. She had sat through enough afternoon-TV talk shows to realize that she had slipped into what was called a "victim mentality." By giving up, she was making it even easier for him to murder her. That wouldn't do. Brush turned her anger away from herself and onto her kidnapper, where it rightly belonged. She wanted to hurt him, to hurt him before he hurt her. She had a weapon; the question was, how to get to it with a gun in her back?

There was a pothole ahead in the dirt road. She steered for it, and when the car lurched into it, she elbowed her purse from the console between the front seats. It spilled onto the floor mat at her feet. She trapped the pepper-spray canister under her left foot to keep it from rolling out of reach.

The man with the gun put out his hand.

Had he seen the pepper spray fall out? she thought wildly. No matter. She had to act as if he hadn't. She leaned forward, grabbed the purse by the strap and handed it back to him.

As he turned to put the purse on the seat beside him, she reached down with her left hand and snatched up the pepper spray, dropping the aerosol can into her lap.

On the left, beside the canal, was a big shade tree with branches that drooped all the way to the ground. He made motions that she should pull over and park under it.

Brush stopped the car and turned off the engine. She had never used pepper spray before, and now her life depended on it. The directions said it would incapacitate a man for more than five minutes. That would give her enough time to get away.

In the rearview mirror, she saw that he was doing something in the back seat. He was bent over, looking at his boots. She thumbed off the safety cap with her left hand and found the nozzle. Glancing down at her lap, she carefully made sure it was aimed away from her face.

She reminded herself to close her eyes when she sprayed, then take the keys, get out of the car and run.

TACHO JABBED the muzzle of the H&K MSG-90 into the woman's ribs, reminding her to sit still, then bent and started to unlace his right boot. He intended to use the car for the rest of the day; he didn't want any blood in it that he would have to explain if he got stopped by the police for a traffic violation. He had already thought up his story in case he was pulled over. He was simply running to the pharmacy for his employer, who was bedridden, and now he was lost. It was sort of an emergency. The woman had a heart condition. He had dashed out of the house without remembering to pick up his wallet.

Yes, sir, Officer. It won't happen again.

Tacho kept his hands down, out of sight of the woman. He didn't want her to see the boot lace stretched between them until it was coming down over the tip of her nose.

The driver's-seat headrest was going to be a problem, he realized. The back of her head was pressed into it. To do the job right, he had to completely encircle the neck, cutting off both blood circulation to the head and air to the lungs. It was going to be harder if he had to strangle her around something. In his experience, though, grandmothers were usually easy to kill, so he decided to give it a try, anyway. After all, there was no help for miles around. If he had to drag her out of the car and crush her skull with the gun butt or drown her in the canal, he still could.

There was no question that she had to die and disappear. He needed the car, free and clear, for six or seven more hours. He had things to do, places to go if he was to avenge the death of Gaspar. No one would start looking for the woman until after noon. By then, it would be too late, even if they traced him to the car.

He snapped the boot lace over the top of her head, over the headrest and under the point of her chin. She let out a gasp of surprise, but before her fingers could get under the lace, he jerked it back hard against her throat, trapping the back of her head against the rest.

She made gagging sounds as he twisted the lace tighter. But she didn't go limp.

This one was going to be tough, Tacho thought. He put the soles of his boots against the back of the driver's seat to gain leverage and bring the big muscles of his thighs into play.

She raised her left hand beside her head. Tacho saw she had something in it and started to turn his face. Then she sprayed him.

The sensation of wet mist on his cheek and the burning

pain on his skin coincided. He couldn't breathe for the fire in his nose, throat and lungs. He couldn't see for the acid in his eyes.

However, instead of completely incapacitating him, it drove him into a frenzy of anger.

He dropped the ends of the boot-lace loop and kicked open the car's rear door. Then, opening her door, he dragged the gasping woman out of the car and threw her onto her face in the dirt.

Tears streaming down his cheeks, he found the ends of the boot lace and finished the job.

Tacho used canal water to try to wash the pepper residue from his skin and eyes. It only seemed to make the burning sensation worse. Then he opened all the car doors and windows. While the car aired out, he lifted the car's trunk lid and removed the spare tire, which he deflated completely. He rolled the dead woman onto her back and put the flat tire on her chest. With some clothesline cord he found in the trunk, he tied the dead woman's wrists together through the wheel's axle hole. Then he lugged her over to the edge of the canal and pitched her in.

He had his transportation.

The next thing he had to do was get some bullets for the rifle.

You could hijack a car with an empty gun, but you couldn't snipe with one.

17

From the log-lined view slit in the hilltop sniper bunker, Rigo scanned the landscape downrange. The bright midday sun reflected off the half-acre pond and the green leaves of the oak trees bordering the two-lane driveway. He caught a movement at the base of one of the trees, and scanned back. One of the Colombians assigned to the fortified foxholes along the drive was urinating against the trunk. Rigo watched as the man fastened up his pants and then climbed into the sandbagged pit.

At least he and Alphonso were in the shade. The two-man belly hide they occupied had been built three days earlier on del Borgo's orders; all four El Salvadorans had participated in the construction. It had a log-and-dirt roof, the latter decorated with living sod, and a sandbagged, log-reinforced firing port. There was room inside the hide for a shooter and a spotter in prone position. Cases of .308-caliber ammunition, food, water and other necessities were stacked at the back of the bunker. Sited among some mature pine and oak trees at the top of the hill, the hide allowed them to cover almost every square foot of the estate's approach and outbuildings. They were all but invisible to aerial surveillance.

Both El Salvadorans had already taken numerous practice shots on man-size targets set up at various distances. They had locked in the range to the top of the lower hill, on their left. They had also nailed down the main house, the cabana, the road, the stables and the one-and-one-quarter-mile exercise track for the Thoroughbreds. They could shoot with confidence anywhere within a six-hundred-yard, 180-degree radius of their hide.

On the other side of the road was a higher hill, but it was more than one thousand yards away, too far for effective countersniping by the enemy.

Rigo swung the spotting scope onto the main house. The building reminded him of one he had seen in a TV show about rich Texans. It was three stories high, with big white columns in front. A fortified foxhole had been dug at the mansion's near corner, manned by a Colombian with an M-16. Rigo scanned on.

Around one end of the stables, he could see into the exercise yard. The blond prostitute was leading a saddleless horse around on a training rope. He zoomed in on her. She had a pouty mouth and very white teeth. As Rigo's mind ran to such things, he immediately began to fantasize what it would be like to be the center of her attention.

Of course, he hadn't been offered her services.

Colonel Suarez came out of the stable door and walked over to the exercise yard's wooden fence. He was wearing a khaki shirt and pants. He said something to the blonde, then ran a hand across her buttocks.

That Suarez alone had enjoyed the privilege of access to the blond woman was something of a thorn in Rigo's side. After all, the colonel hadn't actually done anything to deserve the honor. Since they'd arrived in the States, Suarez had been acting like a spoiled baby instead of an Atlacatl Battalion leader. He refused to get his own hands bloody, but he had spoken to them at length about upholding the glory of their battalion.

Words were cheap.

"Look!" Alphonso said, drawing back from the scope

of the MSG-90 and pointing with his finger. "Over there, at ten o'clock. That's the same plane as before."

Rigo switched to a pair of minibinoculars. The aircraft was the same color and the same make of small, single-engined plane that had overflown them two hours earlier. He couldn't make out the ID number because of the sun's glare. "Maybe it is, maybe not," he replied. "You're getting edgy for no good reason. Even if it is the same plane, that doesn't mean it's interested in us. It could just be coming back from wherever it went."

Though Rigo said this with conviction, hoping to calm his partner, he didn't fully believe it himself. He had a powerful sense that things were quickly coming apart. Considering what had happened in the past twenty-four hours, that feeling was understandable. The mission at Fox Island had succeeded, but it had cost Gaspar his life and Tacho his sanity. The Cay property—the sale of which was supposed to cover their salaries, bonuses, expenses and the cost of their relocation to Costa Rica—had been lost. And now they had been ordered to take up a defensive position on the hilltop. The idea that he and Alphonso might soon be fighting for their lives, as had the Colombians at the Cay, and without an easy escape route, didn't sit well with him at all.

Another thing was preying heavily on Rigo's mind: the prospect of having to face the North American.

Had he not witnessed it with his own eyes at Fox Island, Rigo wouldn't have believed that one man could inflict that kind of damage, that number of casualties. At close range and extreme distance, he was the best the El Salvadoran had ever seen. The shot he had made on Gaspar was nothing short of incredible. And the twenty Colombian gunmen hunkered down at the main house didn't make Rigo feel less uneasy. From the reports of the three who had escaped the Cay the previous night, almost that many had been killed there.

The El Salvadoran snipers had faced skilled enemies before, both in their own country and in Colombia. But before this, they were always the aggressors, offensive players who could choose the time and place of engagement and withdrawal. This situation was different. Their mission was to *hold* position against all comers until further notice, until the cases of ammunition ran out, until del Borgo arranged to get them their money. Rigo and Alphonso weren't going anywhere without their money.

Rigo turned the spotting scope back to the exercise yard. The blonde was leading the horse into the stable. Suarez followed her.

"That lucky bastard," Alphonso said.

"Yeah, lucky," Rigo agreed.

FRANCISCO VERDUSCO, hurtled across the room, landing on his back on an antique Louis Quinze table, the legs of which splintered under his weight, dropping the man and the gold-leaf-decorated tabletop to the floor. As Verdusco struggled to rise, Raffi del Borgo drew a .40-caliber Glock pistol from a holster in the small of his back and pointed it in his face.

Certain del Borgo was going to shoot, and not wanting to be hit by the backsplash of brains and blood, Bud Hylander took a giant step backward. He had never seen the drug lord in such a state of agitation, throwing things and people around the room. He was taking the loss of his Plantation Cay property very hard.

Hylander hadn't known del Borgo in the bad, bad old days—there were, in fact, few surviving witnesses from that time. During the Emerald Wars, sudden, irrational bursts of violence and rage had been del Borgo's personal trademark. Under strain he was reverting to his earlier self.

"I don't want to hear any more excuses," del Borgo told Verdusco. "The next person who makes an excuse to me will die on the spot, whether I need him or not."

Verdusco tested his jaw to see if it was broken, then slowly rose from the floor.

"A very simple operation has been turned into something extremely complicated because you made the mistake of underestimating the opposition," del Borgo said. "I counted on leaving the country today, before anyone had time to connect the killings or guess who was behind them. I counted on the ten million in cash from the Cay property to cover expenses. I'm cut off from all my other sources of money. I'm going to have to remain here in hiding until I can convert some other U.S. property into hard currency. That could take a week or more. You have put us all in jeopardy."

"How was I to know they had the Cay property linked to you?" Verdusco said. "We all thought it was clean."

Del Borgo half raised the Glock. What the man had said bordered very narrowly on being an excuse. However, there was no denying it was true. They had all thought the connection between Rupert Mahoney and del Borgo was untraceable.

"So, are you saying they might have this property under surveillance, as well?"

Bud Hylander chose this moment to step between the two men. "Mr. del Borgo, wait a minute," he said. "I've got excellent connections in the Justice Department and DEA. I'd know if anyone there was onto us, and by now I'd already have been warned. It's what I pay them for. These are the same people who tipped me off before Justice and DEA looked into my 'inheritance' five years ago.

"The other thing is, what happened at the Cay doesn't sound like any federal operation I've ever heard of. Not even Waco, for Christ's sake. They gave the people there *weeks* to surrender. At your place last night, they just moved in and mowed everybody down. I'm telling you, Mr. del Borgo, it wasn't Justice that did that. No way would they risk the bad publicity.''

"So, who's on my case?'' The drug lord reholstered the Glock, much to Verdusco's relief.

"It's not Cali,'' Verdusco said. "Cali doesn't like publicity, either. We do know who one of the participants was. The El Salvadorans said the guy who screwed up the Fox Island thing was part of the R setup. He was the one who okayed them for the sniper work in Colombia.''

"Military? CIA?''

"Apparently not active duty. A mercenary, maybe. At any rate, a freelance operator of some kind.''

"He should have been on the hit list,'' del Borgo said, turning his ring around and around his finger.

"We had no way of knowing that he would be called back in. He would've been very hard to track down. We had to draw the line somewhere.''

"You drew it in the wrong place.''

"Yeah.''

"You two are giving this one man a whole lot of credit,'' Hylander said. "How he could have done all the damage to the Cay? It isn't possible.''

"Since everyone who saw the guy is dead, it's hard to say,'' Verdusco replied.

"We can expect him here?'' del Borgo asked.

Verdusco nodded. "I think so. The longer we stay, the better the chances he'll show up.''

"Call the helicopter pilot,'' the drug lord said. "Tell him I want to leave in half an hour. I will conduct the rest of this business from the air.''

Del Borgo turned to Hylander. "I want you to take out a loan on this place. I need a couple of million in cash by 5:00 p.m. today.''

"That's going to be very hard to do, Mr. del Borgo. Maybe in three days..."

"Haven't you been listening? Don't you understand our position here? In three days this place could be rubble and ashes, too. And we could be dead. All of us, dead. We have to move and move quickly. If you can't get a loan, then cash in some of the livestock. You've always got buyers for that, don't you?"

"Well, uh, sure..."

"Sell one of the Thoroughbred studs, sell all of them if necessary. Just get me the money."

Hylander nodded, his stomach tied up in knots. Prior to this moment, he hadn't experienced any downsides to being a front man for a Colombian drug lord. Everything had always gone smoothly, no worries since he had retired from the force. He had even fooled himself into believing he and del Borgo were partners in the horse farm. The truth was hard to choke down. No part of this place had ever been his. Though he had made it into a highly profitable business, he was nothing more than a caretaker.

"I'll make the calls," he said.

WHEN VERDUSCO HAD DRAWN up a defense of the estate, he had hoped he would never have to use it. There was no way of winning a defensive battle here. He didn't have enough men, and he had no resupply. The best he could do was to hold off an inevitable defeat for as long as possible while inflicting the maximum number of casualties on the enemy.

After what had happened at Plantation Cay the previous night, he knew he had to think siege, up front. If he spread his forces too thin, fully manning all the foxholes he had ordered dug, there wouldn't be enough men left to defend the house from the inside. They would all be destroyed. If, on the other hand, they could manage to keep the enemy out, del Borgo would have enough time to conclude his business.

There was also the question of Verdusco's personal survival.

The Tactician knew that if he could arrange to be encircled, but not crushed, he could then bargain for his own life and the lives of his surviving men.

When he had addressed all the Colombian gunmen in the ranch's bunkhouse earlier in the day, he hadn't let any of this pessimism seep into his speech. He knew his men. They had to believe they could win or they wouldn't fight hard enough to even bring about a draw.

Some of what he had told them was the truth. He couldn't very well lie to them about things they already knew, such as the disaster on the Cay.

"We have to be prepared so that doesn't happen to us," he had said.

They seemed to understand.

From the front porch of the main house, Verusco did a quick check of his deployment. He had four men in sandbagged emplacements along the road. There were two others standing at the double doors of the vehicle-storage barn; two more at the front and rear doors of the stables. All of them were armed with full-auto 5.56 mm assault rifles. In the back of the main house, one man was posted at the tennis court and another at the rear of the cabana house. Inside the cabana house, waiting to escort del Borgo to the helicopter, were six more gunmen.

Verdusco stepped around the corner of the porch. A drug soldier waved at him from a foxhole in the lawn. The man's face gleamed with sweat. And not entirely from the heat. His job was to make early contact with the enemy. With aimed fire he was to delay any intruders so the snipers on the hilltop could pick them off.

Based on what had happened at the Cay, Verdusco knew this man and the others would probably all be sacrificed.

"Stay alert," he said, then he returned to the house.

BRENDA LEE BAKER didn't have to look behind her to know that she was being followed into the stable. The colonel had been bird-dogging her all day. She had gone to bed the night before, fully expecting him to be dead before sunrise. Seeing him still alive this morning had been the most unpleasant surprise she'd had in a long time.

Overnight, things had changed.

Del Borgo hadn't said anything to her. There was no reason to. She already knew.

The disgusting man was evidently still necessary.

Suarez was clearly getting off on the game he was playing. He was trying to make her nervous by hanging around her, making thinly veiled threats, testing to see how frightened she was, a power trip that was supposed to reinforce the idea that she was his to do with as he wished. Even his to kill, if he wanted to.

Baker had no intention of being a murder victim. She also knew that if she showed him her fear, it would only excite him and he would do something to hurt her, perhaps badly.

She couldn't lock the stable door after her.

He followed her in as she returned the horse to its stall.

"Why don't we take a shower together?" he suggested.

"I don't think so."

The colonel didn't like being thwarted by a woman. He reached out and grabbed her by the arm, digging his fingers into her flesh.

"Then get your clothes off," he said. "I'll do you here."

Baker went soft. It was a response made automatic by her martial-arts training: she *seemed* to give in when he pulled her to him. Even though she moved and her weight shifted, her stance remained rooted solidly to the earth.

Suarez didn't notice. He was too busy unreeling a gruesome fantasy in his head.

"Do you know how many *putas* like you I've killed?"

"Ten thousand?" she replied, her expression deadpan. "Twenty thousand?"

He backhanded her across the face.

"Sorry," she said. "I thought you were the major whore killer of the universe."

He hit her again.

She tasted blood. For a guy his size, she decided he didn't really have much of a punch. Her feet shuffled, her long legs scissored, a wave passed under the soles of her shoes. She brought her heel down on his instep, hard enough to feel something crunch.

It made him let go of her arm but made him very angry.

"You little bitch," he growled. "I'm going to feed you your own guts. But first I'm going to skin you alive."

His hand dipped inside his sleeve, then it moved in a blur.

She twisted, blocking with the back of her wrist, making hard contact with something. That something pierced her shoulder, knocking her back against the stall's gate. Baker looked down at four inches of steel sticking out the front of her deltoid; the triangular point of the throwing knife protruded a half inch from the back of her shoulder muscle. The pain was excruciating.

Before she could jerk it out, he was all over her, no longer pulling his punches. He hit her in the face twice, snapping her head back. Baker felt her knees buckling.

He kicked her in the stomach, knocking the wind out of her, then grabbed her injured arm and bent it around behind her back. The contortion forced the muscle to slide against the razor-honed blade, slicing it deeper. The pain dropped her to her knees.

When he lifted her up, it hurt even worse. It hurt so much that the woman couldn't breathe.

Twisting her to face an empty stall, the colonel said, "Now we're really going to have ourselves a party."

18

Bolan inched his way along the foot-deep gully, pulling his Remington sniper rifle behind in a drag-bag. He approached the estate from the north, crawling through the ankle-high pasture grass. The sounds of birds and insects surrounded him. Inside the camouflaged suit, the temperature hovered around 120 degrees.

He had a more difficult stalk than Hawkins, and not just longer. The elevation of the second-highest hill, to his right now as he crept toward the mansion, allowed it a sector of fire that covered most of his approach. He wasn't protected until he reached the slope of the lowest of the three hills, the shoulder of which created a blind spot for the snipers. He knew the El Salvadorans' hide was up on the middle hill somewhere. It had to be. The south-facing side of that hill was six hundred yards from targets coming from the road and the estate's outbuildings, and three hundred yards from the summit of the lowest hill. If they were using the same weapons as before, and there was no reason to expect they had changed, six hundred yards was the maximum distance their rifles could cover.

Bolan carried a lot of gear with him, enough for an all-out assault on the mansion. In that regard he and Hawkins were about even, since Hawkins's gun weighed almost twice what his did.

When the Executioner arrived at the shoulder of the hill, he was a little more than three hundred yards from the main house. Side-scanning infrared during the last fly-by showed no targets on the lowest hill. That was no guarantee that it wasn't occupied, so he moved carefully. He crawled to the cover of some small pine trees on the hillside and rose to a crouch. There, he removed the silenced, camo-wrapped Beretta 93-R from its holster pouch inside the camo suit. With minibinoculars he scanned the grounds below.

Four men with assault rifles sat in the trees along the road. They were in dug-in positions, fortified with sandbags. He marked more drug soldiers at the stable doors and rear of the house, as well as at the entry to a large storage building next to the stables.

It was a token force, which left two possibilities. They were either trying to lure the opposition into a trap to be sprung by snipers or a concealed conventional force, or the men outside the main building were an early-warning device—the Colombians intended to try to hold the house.

Neither tactic was sound.

Bolan cautiously moved uphill. After going through the aerial-recon photos of the hilltop, he had preselected the site of the dummy hide: a small boulder outcrop. He paused below the ridgeline to remove the necessary items from his drag-bag, then he dropped back to his belly and began a tediously slow crawl to the outcrop.

His only protection the camouflage suit, he inched his way into the sights of the snipers' guns. He put his back to the enemy position, concealing what he was doing. Curled up like that, he looked like a big tussock of grass at the base of the boulders. He dug a shallow hole in the soft dirt in front of the outcrop, placed something inside, then covered it again. Then he slowly crawled back to the safety of the ridgeline. A casual observer walking past the outcrop would've missed what the Executioner had left behind, unless he or she accidentally kicked it out of the dirt. The El Salvadoran spotter would certainly miss it from three hundred yards away, unless he had a clue where to look.

Bolan was going to give him that clue.

His actual hide was about sixty feet distant, just over the crown of the hill, out of the line of possible ricochets. The Executioner got into position at the base of an oak tree. He immediately used the Leupold's Mil Dots to estimate ranges to the available targets. He noted the numbers in his head. He had a six-hundred-yard shot to the helicopter, which sat on a flat stretch of mowed lawn on the other side of the estate's pond.

Then a new target presented itself.

A man exited the front of the mansion, running. He rounded the end of the pond and headed for the helicopter at top speed, which was precisely what Bolan wanted.

In the best of all possible scenarios, the Colombian drug lord would try to use the helicopter to escape. Across the road, on the highest hill, Hawkins was already in place with the AMAC. They were in perfect position to cross fire the landing pad.

The chopper's main rotor started up.

There was no sign of del Borgo at the front of the house.

Bolan swung the telescopic sight back on the helicopter. The pilot was throttling up.

The chopper rose into the air with only the pilot on board.

Bolan clicked the Ultra down to a three-hundred-yard zero, then tracked the pilot with the cross hairs as the aircraft turned toward him at 150 feet of altitude and headed right at the three-story house.

His position and Hawkins's on the higher hill shared the same dead spot: the lawn directly behind the cabana house. If the pilot landed the chopper there, they couldn't fire on it. From that takeoff point, the pilot could do a grass-top sweep down the slope, away from the buildings, using them to screen hostile fire until he was out of range.

A decision had to be made.

Bolan released the Remington's safety, hoping to hell Hawkins was making the same one.

EVEN WITH the astronomical telescope he had brought along, Hawkins couldn't locate the El Salvadorans' hide on the south-facing hilltop. That didn't surprise him. From what Bolan had said, these guys knew their fieldcraft.

He had been in his own hide for a little more than ten minutes. In that time he had ranged and logged all visible primary and secondary targets, and he had planned the target sequence he would follow.

As soon as he started shooting, the El Salvadoran snipers would know where he was. The clamshell muzzle brake on the AMAC would leave a telltale muzzle-blast and flash. But that didn't concern him because he was so far outside the effective kill range of the sniping weapons they favored.

Of the two assignments on this mission, his was by far the least risky. It was, however, critical to success. He had to knock out the snipers before they could zero in on Bolan, and he had to do serious damage to the people and structures below, allowing the Executioner to penetrate the buildings, if that proved necessary.

With his naked eye, Hawkins saw the man dash out from between the pillars of the mansion's front entry. Before the pilot reached the helicopter, Hawkins had moved behind the heavily sandbagged AMAC, and had the 32-power scope trained on him.

He adjusted the BDU for a six-hundred-yard range, compensated the aim point for down-angle and fifty extra yards of actual distance to the target, then settled in for a one-shot kill on the front passenger seat, which del Borgo would either have to sit in or pass by to reach the back seats. The butt of the AMAC's adjustable stock didn't rest against his shoulder; in fact, after he made his sighting adjustments, the only part of the weapon he made contact with was the trigger, and that with the pad of his finger. Sandbags and the forestock's bipod legs held the heavy gun in place.

"Goddamn!" Hawkins exclaimed when the chopper took off without picking up a passenger.

Things weren't going to be easy, after all.

He made his decision as the helicopter wheeled away from him, heading for the house. They had to have containment.

Hawkins compensated for the downward angle and the speed of the aircraft, and tightened on the trigger. The AMAC roared.

There was no turning back now.

WITH A NERVOUS AUDIENCE of six of his hired guns, Raffi del Borgo paced back and forth in the living room of the cabana house. The sound of the helicopter starting up didn't ease the drug lord's mind. Five years ago machines counted his money, politicians courted his favor, generals saluted him. Five years ago he could never have imagined himself in this position: running, scared and cash poor, into the unknown. His enemies had hobbled him, ultimately reducing his options to this headlong flight. For a man of power, albeit evil, for a man of pride, albeit in murder and other criminal acts, it was a painful and degrading moment.

And it was about to get worse.

"The helicopter is coming," one of the drug soldiers said from the open doorway.

Del Borgo stepped outside the door and onto the pool deck as the chopper appeared high above the roof of the main house. As it began an angled descent, which would take it over the top of the cabana house to the lawn behind, there was an explosion at the back of the helicopter. With a sudden, terrible grinding noise, the rear rotor flew apart.

The helicopter seemed to hesitate for an instant, then it dropped at a much steeper angle, its fuselage spinning around and around the pivot point of its main rotor shaft. Its forward momentum carried it past the edge of the main house's roof as it plummeted from the sky.

Del Borgo realized with a start that the machine was coming down.

On him.

He threw himself inside the house as the helicopter crashed into the pool. Behind him the blades of the main rotor struck the pool's concrete splash guard. Chunks of flying shrapnel blasted through the cabana windows, bowling over one of the Colombians standing inside.

The dive angle of the helicopter bounced it out of the pool and onto the flagstones. It rolled end over end, its fuselage disintegrating as it thrashed to a stop on the lawn behind the house.

When del Borgo pushed up from the living-room carpet, he got a powerful whiff of aviation fuel; the surface of the pool and the flagstones were slick with it. The man hit by a big piece of rotor blade lay on his back on the carpet. He wasn't moving. Around him in a rapidly spreading ring, purplish blood soaked into the white carpet. The jagged, four-foot length of metal had nearly cut him in two.

The drug lord looked out the cabana's doorway at the scattered wreckage of the helicopter. Its pilot had been thrown clear of the aircraft when it had hit the flagstones and now he sat not ten feet away from where del Borgo stood. The pilot was still strapped into his flight chair, which had been violently separated from the cockpit, via the windscreen. His face was unrecognizable as human, a shapeless mass of blood and bone that sprouted brown hair. The right side of his chest had been blown away from armpit to hip. The fatal injury hadn't happened during the crash. It was clearly a heavy-caliber bullet wound.

For a long moment there was silence as the truth sank in.

Raffi del Borgo wasn't going anywhere.

MACK BOLAN DIDN'T HEAR Hawkins's shot because of the roar of the .300 Winchester Magnum round he had just touched off. As he fought down the recoil wave, recovering the target through his scope, he saw the rear rotor of the helicopter explode into fragments just as it flew over the main house. He knew then that Hawkins had to have fired, because his target had been the pilot. The aircraft autorotated, spiraling down behind the house.

The horrible, grinding crunch of impact rolled up the hillside.

One thing was certain, the Executioner thought. Nobody was going to walk away from that crash.

The Executioner cycled the Remington, closing the bolt on a live round. He knew the snipers would be scanning the hilltop, looking for him. They probably already had the area narrowed down from his first shot, and he was going to help them narrow it down a bit more.

He swung his sights back to the road. The distance to his target was the same, three hundred yards, so he didn't have to adjust his BDC, which saved him a second and cost a drug soldier his life. The Colombian in the foxhole nearest him was standing on top of the sandbagged pit, apparently trying for a better view of the house and accident site. He hadn't made the connection between the gunshots and the crash.

He was about to.

Bolan put the cross hairs even with the man's armpits, adjusted the aim point down for the shooting angle and fired. As the trigger snapped, he pushed the fire control of the remote detonator in his left hand. The Remington bucked hard against his shoulder.

Flicked by a 200-grain finger, the Colombian went somersaulting off the sandbags. A cloud of blood mist hung in the bright air, glistened for a split second, then vanished.

Upslope from Bolan, at the precise moment the .300 Winchester Magnum round sailed away, a small device exploded in the dirt in front of the boulder outcrop. It made no noise to speak of, but flashed and sent a small dust cloud in the air.

RIGO RESISTED THE URGE to scan beyond the corner of the cabana house for wreckage of the helicopter. He had heard two gunshots—one was a big bore, from the sound of it—and knew precisely what had brought the aircraft down. He also had a good idea where one of the shots had come from. He concentrated his spotting-scope search on the closest hilltop, which was a sixth of a mile away and seventy feet lower in elevation than his position. He swept the scope over the crown of the hill, stopping to examine every place he would have chosen for a hide—deep in the sporadic clumps of brush, low in shade of the pine and oak trees, near the small boulder outcrop on the hill's south face.

Rigo knew the hilltop because he had walked it many times in anticipation of this moment. Of course, there was no way he could memorize every bush, every suitable depression in the earth. A man in a well-made camo suit would be almost invisible until the moment of firing. At that instant the flash and blast of the muzzle would give him away.

That was what he and Alphonso eagerly sought, and what they found.

There was a flash and a puff of dust as another gunshot cracked. Rigo recognized the sound of the gun this time. It was the same weapon they had faced at the lake, the gun of Blue Eyes, the cold one.

"Two feet to the right of the tallest boulder," Rigo said, announcing the spot. "He's hiding in the tall grass there."

"Got him," Alphonso said, holding solid on the lump of grass and earth just above where he had seen the flash.

Alphonso fired. Inside the bunker the blast of the .308 shook loose a rain of fine dirt from the low ceiling.

Rigo watched through the spotting scope and caught the shadow of the bullet as it nipped into the waves of mirage rising from the hilltop.

Nothing, no puff of dust as the slug slapped cloth and flesh, no human figure suddenly appearing out of the waving landscape of green, mortally wounded by Alphonso's shot. The bullet simply disappeared into the lush grass.

"You missed."

"Like hell I missed," Alphonso said, pressing his cheek to the stock weld, bearing down for another try. He put the cross hairs a foot closer to the boulder, figuring that the blue-eyed man would try to draw back into solid cover. He touched off a second bullet while Rigo watched the target area.

Again there was no apparent result.

"Maybe he moved," Rigo suggested. "He could be hiding behind the outcrop."

"Impossible," Alphonso said. "If he'd moved, we would have seen him. He isn't there." Then the truth hit the sniper like a snap kick to the gut. "It's a trick, to draw us out. Get down!"

It was already too late.

EVEN BEFORE the El Salvadoran's first shot, Hawkins had his telescopic sight locked in on his general location. He had guessed where they would want to site the hide in order to control the most ground downrange. When the first shot went off, he saw the muzzle-flash through his scope. It forced him to revise the reality his brain had constructed in the view field. What had appeared to him to be a shadow line beneath a fallen log was actually the view-firing port of a sniper's bunker.

He squeezed the sandbag under the AMAC's butt, fine tuning his aim point for the long shot. When the second muzzle-flash confirmed the location of the snipers' hide and the position of the shooter inside it, he released the safety and fell into his breathing rhythm. He couldn't see into the bunker because of the shadow cast by the log, but he could judge the width of the view slit and, from that, the position a rifleman inside would have to take in order to fire on the lower hilltop. Based on this, he set his cross hairs. When he was satisfied, he started to tighten the trigger slack. It broke crisply under his fingertip, and the heavy gun jerked back on its bipod. Seven hundred and nine grains of machined steel death screamed out of the barrel. The muzzle brake eased the punishment of the recoil and raised a visible dust cloud.

Hawkins cycled out the spent casing and inserted another .50-caliber cartridge into the breech. The problem with shooting into a bunker view slit was you never knew whether you'd hit anybody or not.

The solution was to saturate the cover with black-tipped AP rounds, which was precisely what Hawkins proceeded to do, aiming through the slit or just below it.

DEL BORGO KNEW he was in the wrong place if he wanted to survive the afternoon. The cabana was much less defensible than the main house. It had thinner walls, fewer rooms and it was protected by five men instead of more than twenty. The main house meant safety in the short term, anyway, and he intended to have it.

"We are going back to the big house," he told the men.

It was then he noticed one of them had a still-burning cigarette tucked in the corner of his mouth. "Were you born without a brain?" the drug lord snarled. "Put out that damn cigarette! Do it in the sink! There's enough spilled gas out there to burn us all alive."

Del Borgo's plan was to move out in a pack, with two men in front, two in back and one flanking him on the vulnerable side. The human shield was a time-honored tactic in his country. The Colombian gunmen didn't look at all happy about the idea, but they knew they couldn't remain where they were.

There was safety in numbers.

Of a sort.

They could hope some other guy drew the lead sleeping pill.

The booming report of a big-caliber weapon firing between hilltops set them in motion. They rushed out of the doorway, heads and guns up. They had 150 feet of open ground to cross before they reached cover.

They were only one-quarter that distance when the first man in line cartwheeled sideways into the pool.

The sudden movement and splash made the second man turn to look. The guy in the pool floated facedown, surrounded by billowing clouds of red. Somehow the second guy got his feet tangled up, and he fell face-first onto the pool deck.

Del Borgo managed to avoid the man's outstretched legs, but his flanker toppled over them. The drug lord skidded to a stop, dropping to one knee. He wasn't about to be on point with a marksman out there.

The trailing Colombians were beside him in a heartbeat. As the three of them started to move on for the house, as the flanker scrambled up from the deck, his head exploded, sending fragments of skull flying into them so hard that for a terrible instant del Borgo thought he, too, had been hit in the head by a bullet.

"Go! Go!" he urged the survivors.

Even as they ran, another man went down, horribly gut-shot. The shock from the wound was so great that he didn't even writhe from the pain. He just lay there, still breathing, coils of severed innards steaming beside him on the pool deck.

They were less than halfway to the house.

They were never going to make it.

"Back!" del Borgo shouted. He didn't wait for the other two survivors. As he reached the cabana doorway, the man running behind him stumbled and fell. Something thunked into the wall to del Borgo's right. Blood spray-painted a rosy halo around the bullet hole.

Del Borgo once again dived through the doorway. Then he crawled to the cabana's telephone and punched in the code for the vehicle-storage barn. He kicked himself for not thinking clearly under pressure: he should have tried this route first. The Colombian on guard in the storage shed answered on the second ring. His voice quavered.

"Can you drive the limo?" del Borgo demanded.

"Uh, I've never done it, but I'm sure I can. What do you want me to do?"

"I want you to get me the hell out of here," del Borgo said. The car was supposed to be bulletproof. He had paid through the nose for the armor, and it was time to test it. "Drive the limo onto the pool deck," he ordered the man, "and pick me up in front of the doorway. Then we'll cut across the fields to the highway."

"Be there in a minute," the man said, hanging up.

Del Borgo knelt in the ruined living room. The right side of his silk suit jacket was spattered with other men's blood, and the knees of his pants were soaked in it. The big emerald ring was more red than green.

"Goddammit, hurry up!" he shouted out the doorway.

IF ALPHONSO HADN'T PAUSED to warn his spotter, if he had ducked the second the realization hit him, he might have avoided the AP round. It might have slammed startlingly but harmlessly into the boxes stacked at the rear of the hide.

Because he waited to drop his head, Alphonso lost it.

Seven hundred and nine grains of metal hit him below the tip of his nose. The shock wave produced by the bullet, even after one thousand yards of flight, was greater than a .45-caliber round fired point-blank. It turned bone and blood to vapor, which filled the belly hide and coated every uncovered surface inside it.

Rigo breathed the skull and brain mist into his lungs, tasting it, choking on it. He blinked it out of his eyes.

Alphonso had been thrown back from the view slit. He lay rolled up on his side next to Rigo. Between his shoulders, where his head should have been, was an angry red stub of spinal column.

The stub rested against Rigo's leg.

As he jerked away from the contact, another heavy bullet slammed the bunker. When the falling dirt settled, he looked up.

"*¡Madre!*" he moaned, trying to burrow deeper in the earth.

The slug had blasted through the view port's log, splintering out its center as if it were nothing.

It dawned on Rigo that the bunker, though made of rock, dirt and heavy timbers, wasn't cover; it was a death trap.

He manhandled the still-warm body of his partner, lifting it and shoving it halfway out the firing slit, then ducked back down.

Rigo thought that if the countersniper saw he had a confirmed kill, he would stop shooting. The El Salvadoran was too frightened to think clearly. How could a man without a head crawl out of the bunker? Instead of convincing his enemy that the threat had been neutralized, he had just told the countersniper he was still alive.

Another heavy slug zipped through the front of the hide, this one impacting lower, traveling below the log, through the tamped dirt and rock. It missed his shoulder by inches.

"No!" Rigo cried, drawing back into the farthest corner of the hide.

It occurred to him then that he had a choice. He could curl up like a dog and wait for the bullet to find him, or he could try to get through the view slit. If he could clear the bunker, he could run, and if he was running, he had half a chance.

He waited agonizing seconds until the next bullet struck the log, then he jumped up, grabbing the legs of his dead friend and pulling his body back into the bunker. Alphonso's belt buckle caught on the splintered log. As Rigo jerked the corpse clear of the obstacle, pulling the body to him, Alphonso took another hit. The slug entered his upper right chest, shattering his collarbone, then blew his shoulder blade out through the back of his shirt.

Rigo caught the through-and-through bullet in the center of his chest. It divided his heart, turning muscle to bloody jelly in an instant, and blasted a four-inch gap in his spine. He flopped to his back, his limbs jittering the death dance, and Alphonso's corpse fell on top of him.

BOLAN SWUNG the crosshairs onto the running man and fired. A torso hit high in the back sent the drug soldier sprawling onto the pool deck a few feet from the cabana's front door. Meanwhile, del Borgo and the surviving bodyguard slipped to safety inside.

The Executioner tipped the Remington to the side, ejecting the spent brass into the dirt. Even though his main mission was to end the drug lord's life, he had to play by the rules of probability. He had taken shots at the best targets offered him as the entourage tried to cross the pool deck to the main house. He had fired four times and taken out four of the opposition. Four confirmed hits always beat four maybes. And aside from reducing the ranks of the Colombian soldiers, he had kept del Borgo separated from his main force, and therefore at his most vulnerable.

From the steady booms of the AMAC rolling over the grounds, Hawkins was giving the snipers a taste of .50-caliber hell. The El Salvadorans had fired only twice since Bolan had set off the remote charge. He guessed they were too busy—or too dead—to do more shooting in his direction.

Bolan caught movement at the door to the vehicle-storage barn, which sat along one side of the exercise yard, about seventy-five yards from the main house. The door faced his position on the hillside, and as he watched through the Ultra, it slid all the way open from left to right. He cranked the new yardage into the BDC. There was nothing to shoot at yet, so he waited.

An engine started up downrange, revving loudly.

Then the limousine appeared in the barn doorway.

The Executioner found the stock weld and his target in almost the same instant. Through the glare on the windshield, the driver's head was a shadow of a shadow. Bolan put the cross hairs in the middle of the dark place and fired.

He worked the Remington's bolt and brought the gun back on target. The windshield had cracked, but it was still intact. Bulletproof glass. The limo was moving faster now, rolling between the barn and the cover of the main house. He touched off another round, trying to lay it on top of the first. Before he could recover the target and fire a third time, the car slid behind the building.

If the limousine was out of his sight, it was still available to Hawkins. Bolan heard the bark of the AMAC and the solid thunk as an AP slug hammered the car's chassis.

Bolan was ready when the limo reappeared at the corner of the house. It had to cross the open stretch of the pool flagstones to reach the cabana's front door. He fired, aiming at the same spot on the windshield. Whether he actually hit the same place or not, he came close enough. The windshield pebbled and caved in on itself.

The AMAC boomed from uprange, and Bolan saw the car rock on its suspension from the impact of the .50-caliber bullet to the driver door.

The limousine slowed to a crawl. No driver was visible behind the crazed glass of the windshield. The car's front wheels hit the edge of the flagstones, and it started to veer off course. Either the dead driver's foot was still pressing on the gas pedal, or the engine's idle was set high enough to pull the big car along. Instead of angling across the flagstones for the cabana door, it was aimed straight for the swimming pool.

DEL BORGO CRINGED when he saw the limo's windshield give way. He cringed again when the heavy car shuddered from a bullet impact to its left side. At least the thing was still moving, he told himself, and he still had a chance to make a getaway.

"What is he doing?" the drug lord exclaimed. "What is that stupid moron doing?"

The surviving gunman by his side had no answer.

Helpless, they watched from the lower corner of the cabana doorway as the limousine drifted farther and farther to the left. Its front wheels rolled over the splash guard at the shallow end of the pool, dropping the chassis onto the flagstones. Still under power, the rear wheels forced the undercarriage to grind over the splash guard, sliding the car forward past the balance point. The limo nosed down into the water, its rear end up in the air. The back wheels continued to spin for a moment, then stopped as, under the submerged hood, the engine quickly drowned. Fuel from the bullet-ruptured gas tank poured out onto the pool deck.

Stunned, del Borgo shrank back from the dizzying fumes. His options for escape, for survival, had dwindled to two: he had to either fight or die.

WHEN HE SAW THE LIMO tip into the pool, Bolan abandoned his sniper rifle and stripped out of the camo suit. Raffi del Borgo was trapped. It was time to close in and finish the job. He adjusted the ride of his fully loaded combat harness and picked up the sound-suppressed Beretta 93-R, checking the mag to make sure it was full. He picked his way down the grassy slope, moving in a half crouch from one tree trunk to the next. The air felt cool through the sweat-soaked fabric of his camouflage T-shirt and BDU pants. Minus the oppressively hot camo suit, he felt light, quick and deadly.

Aerial-recon photos had shown a hollow area between the house and the foot of the hill, a place where the gently rolling pastureland had collapsed, leaving a scar of bare earth and a depression deep enough for a man to hide behind.

To reach the area, Bolan had to cross an open field in full sight of the soldiers in the house. When a guy in a foxhole alongside the house potshotted at him with an M-16, he wasn't surprised. The bullet sailed wide over his head. He kept on moving, keeping as low as he could.

The guy switched to full-auto and fired a 10-round burst in his general direction.

Bolan didn't bother responding with the Beretta. He was too far away, and he had a lot of ground to cover.

A big bore boomed in the distance, and the shooting from the foxhole stopped.

Hawkins was right on the money, the Executioner thought, zigzagging toward the scar in the pasture.

THE MAN IN THE FOXHOLE had done his job, alerting soldiers in the house that the enemy was advancing.

Through binoculars from a third-story window, Francisco Verdusco watched the lone man run across the field. Though he was big, he moved with the grace of a predator, in smooth, gliding strides. And like a predator closing for the kill, there was a joy in the motion, in the precision of the motion, joy in anticipation of the outcome.

This was the one he had been expecting, Verdusco told himself, the one whose handiwork lay strewed around the grounds of the estate, the one who threatened to destroy everything.

"Shoot!" Verdusco howled. "Kill the son of a bitch!"

Twenty assault rifles poked out from the second- and third-story windows on the north side of the house, each drawing a bead on the running figure.

All opened fire at once.

19

Tacho Ruiz made a right turn and continued cruising around the edge of the town park. The park, like the town, was small: about a block of greenery and trees surrounding a marble war memorial. Gravel paths cut an X through the landscaping. Wrought-iron benches bracketed the children's play area at one end of the park. A couple of mothers sat and watched their kids climb the jungle gym.

Bel Vista, Florida, population 5400, had a nice, sleepy feel to it. Even though people and cars were in evidence, no one was in a hurry. People stopped to talk to each other on the street.

Businesses—retail stores, a café, a doctor's office, a law firm—faced the little park on three sides. Across the street from the war memorial was the town hall and courthouse. Faced with gray stone, the two-story, turn-of-the-century building was topped by a tall bell tower. Metal scaffolding blocked the view of the front of the tower; some repairs were under way, and Tacho could see the workmen behind sheets of clear plastic. Beside the town hall, in a squat, one-story brick building, was the Bel Vista police station. Two empty squad cars sat out front; there were parking spaces marked for two more.

Tacho had put some miles on the stolen vehicle to find this place. It was exactly what he wanted: it was compact in street layout, it had a small population, densely packed and had a tower from which a sharpshooter could dominate the landscape for miles.

He parked in front of Chico's Gun Shop and took a long object wrapped in a coat from the back seat. The front door buzzed when he opened it, alerting the owner that he had a customer.

"How you doin'?" the man behind the glass counter asked. He was bald, fat and dressed in a Kill 'em All, Let God Sort 'em Out T-shirt.

"Okay," Tacho said. His gaze drifted down to the handgun riding in a belt-clip holster above the man's hip. It was a Colt Commander knockoff, 6-shot semiauto, chrome-plated, imitation-pearl grips, probably made in Brazil. The weapon was cocked.

Tacho glanced around the narrow store, finding the usual stuffed deer heads, stuffed birds, hunting-scene posters that advertised ammunition manufacturers. The place smelled of burned coffee, stale cigarettes and gun oil. Under the glass counter was an assortment of handguns, knives and telescopic sights.

"What can I help you with?" Chico said. He nodded at the coat-wrapped package. "Is that a repair job, or do you want to sell it?"

"A repair," Tacho said, removing the coat from the H&K MSG-90.

Chico's eyes lit up. He had read about the weapon in magazines, but had never seen one up close. "Man, that is a sweet-looking gun," he said. "Is it as accurate as they claim?"

Tacho swung the barrel around, pointing it at the middle of Chico's chest. "At this range, I couldn't miss."

"What do you want?"

"Lean over the counter," Tacho told him. "Lay on it and stretch your arms out."

"A holdup!" Chico said. "I don't believe this."

"Stay just like that," the El Salvadoran instructed, holding the H&K extended with one hand, the muzzle aimed at the owner's head as he rounded the glass counter. He lifted the Commander copy from the belt holster. Standing behind the man so he couldn't see what he was doing, Tacho quickly drew back the semiauto's slide a half inch and saw the brass of a .45ACP cartridge case. He set down the sniper rifle and moved to the door.

"Take what you want," Chico said, watching the robber flip over the Closed sign on the door. "I'm insured."

"Thank you, I will," Tacho said. He thumbed off the .45's safety and shot Chico once through the head.

The man slipped down behind the counter, half his face blown away.

Tacho stepped over him to get at the ammunition stacked along the back wall. He took all the .308 bullets, even the non-Match loads, and dumped them into a knapsack he found behind the counter. Then he examined the handguns and binoculars under glass.

The wheelguns he considered useless; he concentrated on the semiautos, removing a 9 mm Beretta and a Smith & Wesson, both with high-capacity, staggered-row box magazines. He found shells for them along the wall and quickly loaded both guns and a pair of extra magazines. Dropping the Beretta in the knapsack, he tucked the Smith & Wesson into his waistband. He added a pair of high-powered binoculars and four more boxes of 9 mm bullets to the bag, which was starting to bulge from the load.

As he retrieved the H&K, he decided that the weapon deserved a hard-shell case and put it in one that Chico had on display. He closed the shop door behind him and moved gingerly to his car.

After backing out of the parking space, he made another tour of the perimeter of the park. This time he noticed the small yellow sign that indicated a school-bus stop.

Better still.

He pulled up in front of the town hall and parked. No one stopped him or gave him a second look as he climbed the steps with the hard-shell case. It could've been a saxophone for all they knew.

There was no security checkpoint inside. The building had an old, motheaten feel to it—the marble floor was worn from foot traffic, the woodwork stained dark, the light fixtures ancient. Tacho walked toward the staircase. There was gold lettering on the wooden doors: Assessor, Records, Utilities, Planning.

At the foot of the stairs was an old-fashioned sign on a wooden post that said Mayor. A golden arrow pointed up.

Tacho climbed to the second story and found the mayor's office. He opened the door and entered a receptionist area with a high service counter. He set the gun case on it. At the back of the room was another door, this one with a frosted-glass window that displayed the word Mayor. Someone was inside. Tacho could see a tall figure moving behind the glass.

"Yes?" said the woman sitting behind the computer screen. She was in her early thirties with dyed blond hair. She wore large gold earrings and blue eye shadow.

"Is the mayor in today?"

"Do you have an appointment?"

"Yes," Tacho said, showing her the pistol.

The woman's face dropped. "Oh, Lord," she said, raising her hands, though he hadn't asked her to.

"Let's go see the mayor." He waved her up from her chair and marched her to the office door.

The mayor, in a short-sleeved white shirt and no tie, turned from a chart thumbtacked to his wall. He was a tall, rangy man with receding gray hair and a prominent Adam's apple.

"I'm sorry, John," the secretary-receptionist blurted. "I couldn't do anything."

"That's okay, Wanda," the mayor said, his eyes locked on to the muzzle of the gun. "You did the right thing."

Looking up at Tacho, he said, "What is this about?"

"You wouldn't understand," Tacho told him. "Do you have any tape?"

"Tape?" the secretary said.

"For sealing packages."

She glanced at the mayor, her eyes full of fear. He nodded to her. They had no choice but to obey the man.

She showed Tacho where they kept supplies. He selected a roll of fiber-reinforced tape and quickly bound their wrists behind their backs. Then he ordered them to stand facing the wall while he took the H&K from its case. He slipped the sling over his shoulder.

"How do we get up into the tower?" he asked.

The mayor turned his head and saw the scoped rifle. That and the request clicked in his head. He visibly sagged. He knew what was about to happen. "Look," he said, "whatever you're mad at, we can fix. Is it the planning department? Do you feel they've treated you unfairly? We can review their decision. I have the authority to reverse whatever they did to you."

Tacho didn't respond.

"Whoever messed with you in this city's bureaucracy," the mayor went on earnestly, "I'll make them sorry. I promise you."

"I don't live here," Tacho said.

The mayor blinked.

"Let's go," the El Salvadoran told them, waving the gun toward the door.

20

Bolan intended to circle around the outbuildings and come up on the cabana house from the rear. The fusillade of autofire from the mansion's upper stories changed his plans. Bullets rained all around him, thudding into the earth. Out of the corner of his eye he glimpsed the muzzle-flashes and clouds of gun smoke drifting from the windows. He couldn't count how many guns because he was moving too fast over the grass. But there were a lot of Colombians unloading their weapons at him as fast as they would cycle. They had a good angle on him from the third floor, so he couldn't just go facedown in the pasture. Even though they were three hundred yards away and using iron sights, they weren't shy about using up the ammo.

He had to run or be struck down.

With that many guns popping off, one thing was certain: evasion—zigzagging, speed changes and the like—was wasted effort. All the fire was unaimed. A hit, if and when it came, would be random, due to the number of shots being sprayed at him. It was like running through a rainstorm and trying not to get hit by the drops.

Only, in this case, the drops were lethal.

High-kicking, his arms pumping, he sprinted for the scar in the pasture's green carpet.

Maybe it was the excitement of being in the middle of all those guns free-firing on automatic, or the clouds of white smoke that momentarily obscured the running target, but the Colombians missed him. The gunfire grew ragged as, one after another, they had to replace empty magazines. That they had failed to drop him with so many shots fired made them even more anxious.

As he closed on the hollow, the last volleys of autofire impacted sixty feet beyond him.

Bolan dived for the depression in the earth. As the ground jumped up at him, he tucked into a tight shoulder roll. The Beretta came up first, clear of the dirt, ready in his fist.

The gunfire from the house stopped. When it resumed, it was only an occasional select-fire pop. The Colombians were finally calming down and getting the range, though. Puffs of dirt kicked down on him from the lip of the scar.

He took a moment to catch his breath, then prepared to break from cover and go the rest of the way. All he needed was a seam to work with.

He mentally urged Hawkins to do his stuff.

THE CHORUS of automatic fire from the mansion was the answer to del Borgo's prayers. He didn't hesitate; he knew what to do. He punched the gunman in the shoulder with the butt of his Glock, then shoved him out the doorway ahead. "Move! Move! Move!" he shouted.

They dashed across the devastated patio, slipping on the spilled fuel, jumping the dead bodies and metal debris.

With all the guns going off in the mansion, it was impossible to tell if they were still under sniper fire. Neither of them was hit, however, and they reached the safety of the house's back wall. Del Borgo opened one of the double French doors that looked onto the pool.

"Don't shoot! Don't shoot!" he cried, shoving the soldier into the house ahead of him. He didn't want to meet up with an overanxious gunman who might shoot before verifying his target.

Only a few guards were posted on the ground floor, at the front and rear entrances.

"Where's Verdusco?" Del Borgo asked the first man they came across.

"Upstairs, along with everybody else," the soldier replied.

Del Borgo vaulted the stairs three at a time. He arrived on the top story just as the gunfire began to dwindle. He looked into doorways until he found his top lieutenant, along with a half-dozen others, in the mansion's master bedroom suite. "Did you get the bastard?" he demanded.

"There's no way of telling yet," Verdusco replied. "We'll know in a minute, when the smoke clears."

Empty cartridges littered the carpet in amazing numbers. Even as del Borgo noted this fact, one of the Colombians stepped away from the windows, slipped on a shell and ended up on his butt on the floor.

"Sweep up those spent casings," del Borgo ordered. "They're a goddamned hazard."

Even Hylander had gotten into the act. The muzzle of his M-16 still smoking, he turned from the window and smiled at the drug lord. "We got that puppy, but good," he said.

"Do you see a body?" Verdusco asked, scanning the field with binoculars.

Del Borgo took a pair of binoculars from one of the soldiers and looked for himself. He lowered them and said, "I don't see a body out there."

"He could have fallen in that pit," one of the Colombians ventured. "He could be laying in there, dead."

Del Borgo grimaced. "Yeah, and he could be laying in there alive, too."

"You got the bullets," Verdusco told his men. "Use them!"

The soldiers at the master-bedroom windows switched to select fire and began plinking away at the dirt mound.

"At least they've got the range," del Borgo said, looking through his binoculars. "If the bastard pops up out of that hole, he's going to get a bullet in the head."

THE SOUND OF GUNFIRE coming from the house drew Hawkins's immediate attention. He turned the astronomical spotting scope in that direction, found the sandbagged foxhole and saw the man firing from inside it. He raised the scope and saw Bolan making a mad run across the open field. The shooter was protected from horizontal return fire from the road and the fields by the layers of piled sandbags, but Hawkins was looking down on him. He had the angle.

Hawkins quickly moved the AMAC into position to fire on the house. As he did so, the guy in the foxhole switched to automatic. The distance to the mansion was the same as to the sniper nest, one thousand yards. So, he didn't have to change anything; all he had to do was adjust the aim point for the shooting angle and fire.

The thirty-six-pound rifle bucked hard, hopping a bit on its bipod because he'd hurried in packing the sandbags on its feet. He recovered the target in time to see the man's arms fly up and the M-16 sail out onto the lawn.

End of threat.

Before Hawkins could unlock the AMAC's bolt, the full-auto attack broke out from the upper story of the house. He closed the bolt and swung up his aim point. Because they were on the other side of the house from him, he couldn't see the windows the men were firing from. But he had examined the architect's plans; he knew where the windows were relative to the attack angle he had on the house.

Shooting through wood shingle and masonry was no problem for the big rifle, especially with the M-2 AP round he was using. The M-2 would penetrate one-third of an inch of face-hardened armor at fifteen hundred yards.

Hawkins put the cross hairs on the first window from the left corner of the front of the house, aiming for the right-hand edge of its window frame, and fired. He didn't bother to check his bullet-fall—it was close enough—but levered the bolt back and rammed home another AP round. He moved his aim point a foot to the right and fired. Again without pause, he reloaded.

Hawkins hit the corner of the house, then moved on. He had no doubt, as he punched holes farther and farther to the right, that the bullets were traveling through everything between them and the far wall. He was shooting through three, maybe four rooms by the time he ran out of house on the right.

The AMAC's barrel was hot, and he'd lost his fine-tuned zero, but he could still hit the house and that was all that mattered. He couldn't hear any more gunfire coming from the house between his own shots, which was a good sign.

Hawkins began to shoot random holes in the front of the house, angling them through to hit the north-facing wall. Occasionally he dropped his aim point to penetrate the second story. He worked like a machine, knowing that Bolan's life depended on the havoc the AMAC was creating inside the mansion.

THE FIRST .50-CALIBER BULLET that sailed through the third-story wall didn't hit anyone, but it froze them in place. Half the inside window frame and a fist-sized chunk of wall disappeared in front of them, and a hole the size of a quarter appeared at belly height in the side wall.

Then they heard the boom.

"Get down," Verdusco said.

The Colombians and Bud Hylander knelt by the windows.

"What kind of gun is that?" the former Miami cop asked.

He got his answer when the next AP round punched through the wall. It caught him high on the right side of the chest, lifting him from the crouching position he was in and hurling him out through the open window.

They watched his bare feet disappear over the sill. The moaning sound he had made as the breath had been driven from his body still hung in the room, a soft echo.

He'd been blown right out of his deck shoes.

Then, way out in the middle of the field, something moved.

"Jesus, the bastard's still alive!" one of the Colombians cried.

Before anyone could raise a weapon toward the running man, another bullet spranged through the front wall. This one took an even more wicked track. It sliced through one gunman's side, turning his intestines to mush, exited his other side and went through a kneeling man's thigh. Then it passed through the side wall. The first guy died from shock before he hit the floor. The second guy had a new joint in his leg, in the middle of what was left of his thigh.

Blood was spurting everywhere.

Del Borgo had witnessed enough. There was no fighting a gun that you couldn't see, a gun that could do that to a human body. Without a word he ran from the room. He jumped the stairs as another heavy bullet thudded against the mansion's facade. Above him he could hear Verdusco shouting orders to his men, trying to get them to follow him out of the line of fire.

BOLAN LET HAWKINS soften up the Colombians with the AMAC before he made his move on the house. After a half-dozen AP rounds had perforated the building, nobody was shooting in his direction anymore.

He knew now that there were a lot of men in the mansion, too many to ignore. He had to make a change in plans. With that many opponents at his back, he couldn't go for the cabana. He had to face them in the big house and kill them there. And he had to hope that Hawkins could get containment on the principal target, Raffi del Borgo, should he manage to slip the noose and make a break for it on foot across open country.

The Executioner cut over the field to the corner of the house without coming under fire. There was a body on the ground under the third-floor windows that had been used as gun ports. The man's lungs had been blown out through his back. The north-facing side of the building was pocked with scores of big bullet holes.

He entered the back of the house through an unlocked first-floor window, slipping through it and dropping to the carpeted floor. It was a library. In the distance Hawkins's gun shots still boomed at regular intervals, the chiming of a .50-caliber Big Ben. The concentrated fire on the upper story of the house would force the gunmen down to Bolan, reducing the amount of house he had to sweep clean.

Outside the library door, he heard male voices. The Spanish was quick and agitated.

He waited until they hurried past, then cracked the door open.

Two Colombians were mounting the broad, formal staircase that led up to the second floor. He stepped out into the hallway and slammed them with a pair of tribursts. The silenced 9 mm rounds hammered them into the stairs. They slid down the steps, their faces bouncing on the treads, and ended up in a tangled heap at the bottom.

From the floor above, Bolan heard shouts and screams, and heavy footsteps running his way. He darted to the far side of the staircase, out of view of the men charging down it.

When the Colombians saw their compadres dead at the bottom of the stairs, they halted abruptly.

Bolan already had the frag grenade out, the pin pulled and was counting down the seconds. He tossed the bomb over the banister and took cover. It exploded in the middle of the cluster of Colombians, sending them flying. One of the men flipped over the stair railing and landed hard on his back in front of the Executioner, his M-16 still clenched in his fists.

He never got the chance to use it.

Bolan shot him once in the temple, whirled and charged up the steps.

Of the other two men caught in the grenade blast, one was clearly dead, his chest and face torn apart. The other guy showed signs of life as he sat on the stairs, trying to raise his autopistol.

Bolan shot him point-blank and stepped over the corpse.

He paused at the first-floor landing. The single staircase split in two, branching in right angles to the first flight of steps. He looked up. The stairwell opened all the way to the third-floor ceiling.

Somebody was looking down at him from the second-floor railing. Autofire chattered as he drew back, slugs ripping up the Oriental rugs on the landing.

Bolan primed another grenade and tossed it up, bouncing it off the second-story ceiling and onto the second floor. The blast brought the Colombian crashing down onto the first-floor landing, the impact leaving the man's neck bent at an unlikely angle.

The Executioner slapped a fresh clip into the Beretta and backed up the flight of stairs.

A head appeared behind the second-floor banister and a gun barrel poked between the rails.

Bolan fired twice, driving the gunner back, making the gun drop. For a moment everything was still. Then blood oozed between the railings where the man had gone down. It drooled over the edge of the floor, dripping down to the first-story landing.

The Executioner swept his sights over the rails and, seeing no other threats, advanced. His grenade had blown out part of the ceiling and started a small, smoky fire in the carpet. Nothing moved along the corridor.

But he knew there were more hardmen, and that they were close.

LOOKING AROUND HIM, Francisco Verdusco could see the fear in the eyes of his men. He could taste it in his own mouth.

The opponent they faced wasn't human. He made no mistakes. He operated at a speed and with an intensity that they couldn't match. And he was at the other end of the second-floor hall.

The only thing they had on their side, the Tactician realized, was sheer numbers, and they wouldn't have them for long at the rate things were going. If any of them was to survive this terrible afternoon, he had to get some fire going in their bellies. He had to show them a plan and make them carry it out.

"He's going to sweep the house, room by room," Verdusco said. "He's looking for del Borgo, looking to kill him, but he'll kill every one of us that he finds. We can't let him divide us up. We have to stay together, to fight him together. Together we can trap this guy." He stared at each of the ten faces in turn. "We've got enough guns here to turn him into hamburger," he said with conviction.

Some of the soldiers looked doubtful. The rest looked shell-shocked. Fresh in their minds were images of the men they had left on the third floor, their body parts torn away by .50-caliber bullets.

Verdusco had to lay it on the line for them. "If we don't

trap this bastard,'' he said, ''he's going to kill us all. Understand?''

''What do we have to do?'' one of the soldiers asked.

''We'll wait until he enters a room, then all move into position to cover the doorway. When he tries to make an exit, we blow him straight to hell.''

''Who's going to volunteer to stick their head out the door?'' one soldier asked. ''Not me.''

''Get ready to move when I say so,'' Verdusco told them. He pulled a small mirror from his pocket. It had a telescoping metal handle, which he fully extended. Then, edging the room's door open, he pushed the mirror into the hall. By shifting the angle, he could see the entire corridor.

The man was there, moving fast and light from one side of the hallway to the other, near the railing of the stairwell. He opened a door and disappeared into a room.

The Tactician drew back his own door and slipped into the hall. He took the lead because he knew his men wouldn't leave the temporary safety of the room if he tried to stay at the rear of the assault. He waved them out after him, pointing at the door their enemy had gone through. Quickly and soundlessly, the Colombians took up firing positions along the hallway, in doorways, behind the railing.

There were eleven guns pointed at the doorway Mack Bolan had entered, eleven guns cocked and waiting.

RAFFI DEL BORGO silently cursed his terrible luck.

For an instant he'd had a clear shot at the tall man as he had backed up the stairs to the second floor. But he had moved so quickly, by the time del Borgo got the sights of his Glock lined up, he was aiming at a foot in a black ballistic nylon shoe.

Then he was aiming at nothing.

Del Borgo could have tried to shoot him in the ankle,

but he held back. It was a difficult shot under the best of circumstances. If he missed...

The consequences of missing were scattered all around him, leaking their bodily fluids into the carpets.

Del Borgo considered his remaining options as he held the pistol in both hands, covering the stairs in case the tall man decided to come back down. He could try to run for it on foot, without risking a face-to-face with the tall man, but there was another gun out there and an equally skilled marksman behind it. The chances of escape weren't good. Success or failure aside, the drug lord felt the need to make a corpse of the man who had ruined all his plans, who had turned him from royalty in exile into a hunted animal and had made him afraid to take a shot.

The drug lord slowly mounted the stairs.

The tall man had to die.

BOLAN HAD NO CLUE what tipped him off. It was something he sensed at a subconscious level, an uncomfortable pressure, a weight of bodies, all closing in on him. He had already finished sweeping the bedroom when he first felt it. The door to the hallway was open behind him. Through it, he could see no movement.

He listened, but there was no sound, except for the moaning of the wounded.

Still, something was wrong.

Silently he slipped a leg over the sill of the open window, unlimbering a small grappling hook and line from his harness. He leaned way out and tossed the hook through the open window of the room next door, the one he had just finished checking. He threw the hook in far enough so it didn't clunk on the window frame, and it landed with a soft thud on the carpet.

Bolan quickly snugged up the hook with the line, making its razor-sharp prongs dig into the plasterboard. Then he launched himself out the window on an extremely short lead. The soft soles of his shoes padded against the side of the house, slowing the speed of his downward arc. He climbed hand-over-hand up the knotted rope and into the adjoining room.

He gave the room's open door a wide berth, coming up along the wall on its far side. He peered out. Sure enough, the Colombians had set up an ambush in the hallway. They were so intently focused on the room they'd seen him enter, they didn't glance in his direction. Because of the steep angle, only one man had a clear view of him in the doorway, and he wasn't looking.

Bolan drew back from the door. He pulled three grenades from his combat harness, the last frag and two concussion bombs, and set them on the carpet in front of him. He dumped the half-spent clip in the Beretta and inserted a full one. Then he armed all three grenades, carefully letting the safeties plink off at the same instant. Keeping well inside the room, he underhanded out the door, throwing them high for maximum blast effect.

The hallway rocked from the multiple detonations.

Bolan counted three, then cleared the door, the Beretta on point and triple-firing in his fist.

VERDUSCO DIDN'T SEE the grenades fly out the door, so the explosions and the pain came as a complete surprise to him. Deafened by the noise, blinded by the blast and heat, he instinctively staggered back, away from the source of the hurt.

His men were dying, and he knew they were dying because the predator walked among them.

Autofire raged in the hallway. In the enclosed space, the noise penetrated even his battered ears and thudded against his flesh. His soldiers were blind-firing in panic. Verdusco felt the wall against his back and let himself slide down it to a sitting position on the floor.

The gunshots quickly stopped.

He raised his own M-16, only to feel a sudden, heavy resistance, a weight on the barrel that twisted the weapon to one side.

"Damn you to hell!" he yelled as he felt the searing touch of the Beretta's muzzle against his cheek.

Then his life ended.

BOLAN WADED into the hallway, into the chaos of grenade smoke and the stench of blood and burning wool carpet, the 93-R hammering out triple beats. Everything that moved was a legitimate target.

A figure slid away from him. Nine-millimeter slugs cut the smoke, driving the gunman into the wall. He bounced off the unyielding surface and fell forward. Without raising his hands to protect his face, he hit the floor, dead, his feet kicking up behind him, his legs rubbery and limp.

Above the railing a Colombian waved his assault rifle, firing wildly into the ceiling. Bolan drilled three bullets into the side of his neck, hurling him sideways and down.

Two more drug soldiers, blinded by the grenade blast, were shooting at nothing, firing full-auto, face front.

He advanced on them from the side, stitching 9 mm lead across a chest-high arc. He chopped down the men, knocking them over like bowling pins.

Beyond their tangled legs, the two gunmen closest to the frag when it blew were piles of bloody, burning rags.

The soldiers farther down the hall were in better shape.

At least they still had heads.

Bolan braced the Beretta against a door frame and, with a single shot, sent a fleeing man into a crashing dive that ended at the base of the wall.

As the smoke in the corridor lifted, the Executioner saw

that one man on the floor remained alive. He recognized the face from the DAS mugshots. It was del Borgo's field general, Francisco Verdusco.

Blood streaming from his ears and eyes, the man sat with his back to the corridor wall, his assault rifle out in front of him.

As Bolan bent down and caught the barrel in his left hand, Verdusco yelled something at him. The Executioner couldn't understand the words. He didn't ask the Colombian to repeat them. He shot him dead, letting the body flop back onto the floor.

As he rose, gunfire raged at him from the top of the stairway, a flurry of wild single shots that channeled the wallpaper and broke out the windows at the end of the hall. Bolan fired an answering triburst and ducked into an open doorway.

The gunfire ceased.

BRENDA LEE BAKER awoke to the sound of automatic-weapons fire. She lay in the straw of the stall, her blouse and riding pants cut and slashed into so many strips that she might as well have been naked. Only her knee-high, leather riding boots remained intact. Between the cuts in her clothing, her skin was marked with thin lines of red where Suarez's blade had sliced too deeply.

She tried to move, and the pain in her shoulder made the stable ceiling spin crazily. She had to close her eyes or pass out again. When the feeling passed, she reached out to touch herself and discovered that the spike Suarez had driven through her muscle had been removed. He had either pulled it out while she was unconscious, or pulling it out made her unconscious, she couldn't remember.

On the other side of the stall, Suarez was taking off all his clothes. He folded his shirt and socks and placed them out of harm's way on top of the stall's wooden railing.

"What's happening out there?" she asked, hoping to divert him from whatever ugliness he had in mind.

"Everyone's dying," he said, stepping out of his trousers. He made neat creases in the pants legs before draping them over the fence rail. Then he plucked the Devil Dart from the rail post and approached her in his black low-rise briefs. "You're dying, too. Can you feel it?"

"You can still get away," she told him. "If you go now, before the others are killed, you can escape."

"Then I'd miss the fun. I've been so looking forward to this." He waved the bead-blasted knife in the air, then hunkered down in the straw, five feet from her.

"Whoever's attacking the farm, they'll kill you, too, when they find you," she said.

"So you and I will die together, or not far apart," he said, making a quick, half-hearted slash at her with the knife.

She jerked her legs back, out of his reach. In the past she had had to deal with tough clients. Some of the men had been strange indeed, brutal even, but she had weathered them all. Truth was, at no time had she believed that her life was in peril.

Unlike now.

The glazed look in Suarez's eyes had a strange effect on her. She felt almost paralyzed. Was there something she could say to him that would deter him from his mission? She forced herself to think, but she came up empty. Okay, if the bastard intended to kill her, there was no way she was going out without a fight.

Baker let her hand slip from her knee to the top of her right boot. She didn't reach inside it. He was still too far away. Umberto, gentle Umberto whom she had serviced under del Borgo's orders, had been adamant about the distance—or lack of same—that was required.

Umberto, the tender Colombian assassin, had given her a special gift, which, up until now, she'd had no use for.

Now it was all that stood between her and a horrible death.

HAD RAFFI DEL BORGO been less cautious, he would have been caught in the hand-grenade explosions that racked the second-story hall. As it was, he was neither blinded nor maimed, although he did sustain a small cut across his right cheek from shrapnel. Rocked by the blast, he ducked and covered, then, hearing the all-out gunfire, moved up the stairs.

As he cleared the middle of the staircase, he could see a tall figure on the floor above, slipping through the smoke. The drug lord climbed higher and saw the muzzle-flashes of the enemy's weapon as he fired point-blank into the heads of the stunned drug soldiers. It was killing like none the Colombian had ever seen, machinelike in speed and efficiency, utterly contemptuous of the possibility of return fire, terrifying to witness.

Del Borgo waited until he had a clear shot, until the man bent to administer yet another coup de grace, then, raising his Glock, he fired every round in the magazine.

When the weapon locked back empty, and a flurry of answering fire gnawed at the banister railing next to his head, he dropped below the line of sight.

He hadn't killed the man—maybe he couldn't *be* killed.

Del Borgo decided he had spent enough time, energy, money and manpower trying to end the man's life. Dropping the gun, he ran down the stairs to the first floor.

He could always pawn his emerald ring, he thought as he jumped the bodies heaped on the floor, pawn the ring and get enough cash to make Switzerland by himself. He couldn't travel in style, but he could get the hell out of that maniac's reach.

He ducked out the French doors that bordered the pool. Keeping low, he rounded the up-ended rear of the limousine.

"Hey!" a voice from the mansion called out to him.

Despite himself, del Borgo turned back to look.

The tall man stood in an open second-story window. He didn't have a gun in his hand, the drug lord noted with relief. Then the tall man's arm moved and something small and dark came flying toward him.

There was no time to run, no place to run.

The flash grenade detonated with a blinding glare. The heat of the explosion ignited the aviation and auto fuel on the pool deck in a terrible air-sucking whoosh.

Raffi del Borgo danced in a lake of fire.

THROUGH THE WAVES of black smoke, Bolan watched the drug lord burn. His arms flapped, and he hopped wildly about. Though del Borgo had dealt misery to untold thousands, the Executioner knew the man was suffering a horrifying death. He unleathered the Beretta and fired off a mercy round.

The black figure amid the writhing flames went suddenly stiff, then toppled into the fiery swimming pool.

Flames licked up the side of the house, forcing Bolan to step back from the window. On the other side of the pool, the cabana house was already completely engulfed in flames.

It was time to search for stragglers.

The Executioner exited the house and ran for the stables. As he approached the stable door, he heard a series of high, shrill screams.

He checked the clip in the 93-R, making sure it was full before slipping through the door.

The screaming continued from the far end of the building. He advanced toward its source, keeping close to the stalls. Then he heard a popping sound, like a muffled firecracker.

The screams stopped, as if cut off by a switch.

He hurried forward, the Beretta up and ready.

In one of the stalls on the right, a blond woman, her clothes cut to shreds, stood over a kneeling, naked man. In her hand she held a belly gun, a palm-sized, blue-steel .22 automatic. She held the muzzle of the pistol pressed into the man's eye socket.

She fired the gun again and again, and every time she fired, the man's head jerked back.

Six times she shot him through the eye. And when the gun was empty, she stepped back and let his body fall to the straw.

It was only then that she saw Bolan.

She turned the pistol on him and snapped the firing pin on an empty chamber six more times.

He stepped forward and easily took the gun from her. She didn't resist. He tossed the weapon into the straw.

Bolan looked down at the dead man, recognizing him from the Stony Man briefing as the El Salvadoran military liaison, Lieutenant-Colonel Suarez, a man who had supposedly perished in a helicopter crash in his own country. This was the traitor who had sold out R to the Medellín cartel, the coward whose greed had cost so many good people their lives.

The blonde had shot him seven times. The first shot, which Bolan hadn't heard, the horrible wound that had caused the man to scream, was down between his legs. The tops of his thighs were smeared with blood.

"Are you all right?" he asked the woman.

She nodded.

"Are you cut?"

"Not badly," she said, glancing down at herself. "God,

I'm a mess." Her whole body started to tremble uncontrollably.

Bolan found a blanket and draped it over her shoulders. "They're all dead," he said as he escorted her out into the bright sunlight. "Wait over by the exercise track. Keep yourself wrapped up in the blanket. Help will be here soon. You'll be okay."

He gave her a gentle push in the right direction and turned away. He didn't look back. He walked past the front of the burning mansion, then cut across the green fields, retracing his steps.

On the side of the lowest hill, where he had left them, he found his Remington and the camo suit. He began to repack his gear, preparing for the flight out.

The sound of a helicopter approaching from the southwest made him straighten. Bolan shielded the sun from his eyes and scanned the horizon for Grimaldi.

21

Hal Brognola and the members of the Stony Man Farm cybernetics team sat transfixed by the live TV coverage of a real-life tragedy in progress. Every station on the computer center's bank of television screens carried the story of Bel Vista, Florida, a small town savaged by a lone gunman.

The situation had been "unfolding" for a little more than three hours. As Stony Man had been monitoring all local and national broadcasts, they were aware of what was happening as soon as the initial local-news bulletin scrolled across the bottom of a screen.

Because sniping incidents weren't that common, and because this sniper was good, right away they knew who it was: the monster who had left the message in blood at Plantation Cay. All they could do was sit and watch as things deteriorated.

The chronology up to that point was still sketchy, but it appeared that sometime before one-thirty in the afternoon an armed man entered the town hall and took the mayor and his secretary hostage. He then made them climb into the bell tower, which was under major repair. On the way he took at least three workmen as additional hostages.

When he heard this, Brognola had put two and two together and deduced that the Salvadoran had used the workmen to sandbag the inside of the tower with bags of cement from the construction area. Subsequent helicopter fly-bys had confirmed the stacking of the one-hundred-pound bags around the four tower window openings. Three of those openings were blocked by louvered wooden panels; the fourth was open, due to the on-going repairs. The slats on the louvers were set so wide apart that the sniper could poke his barrel and scope out and shoot through them.

According to the currently accepted timeline, the sniper was in the tower with the hostages for more than half an hour before he fired his first shot and made his first kill.

He took out a city cop as the man tried to cross from the park to the station house. His body still lay, facedown, in the street.

Apparently no one connected the gunshot with danger for a few minutes. A small crowd gathered around the fallen policeman.

The sniper casually picked off a handful of other pedestrians, including the district-court judge hurrying back to the town hall for the afternoon session. After the judge was shot, the people in the town center got the picture and ran for cover.

About that time, the school bus pulled up at the stop alongside the park.

The bus driver didn't know what all the commotion was about, or maybe there was so much commotion inside the bus he didn't notice that people were hiding behind cars. The sniper shot him dead through the windshield, then proceeded to plink away at the bus, breaking out the windows, perforating the steel skin, while the trapped children screamed in terror. They couldn't touch the lever that opened the bus door without stepping into the line of fire and going very near the ruined head of the driver.

The four city cops on duty, unaware of the hostages that had already been taken, opened fire on the tower with their service revolvers. As they were reloading, a limp human form fell out of the tower and landed on the town hall steps. It was one of the workmen.

Someone found out about the mayor and the others, and spread the news to law enforcement. The cops withdrew without firing any more shots.

When the sniper realized the kids weren't going anywhere, he turned his attention on cars moving on streets and people in their yards up to six hundred yards from the tower. He worked methodically, killing everyone he could.

The media crews arrived about the same time as the Justice Department strike and hostage-negotiation teams. Live video coverage started with the rescue of the children from the school bus.

And more on-air tragedy.

The Justice strike team commandeered an armored car making a pickup at a local supermarket. They drove it onto the sidewalk, pulling it up next to the bus's front door, blocking the sniper's view of the exit. The strike team tried to coax the kids into opening the door from the inside, but they were too scared to move. The dead driver lay sprawled over the steering wheel. Finally one of the strike team crawled through a back window and up the aisle to reach the door controls.

The Salvadoran was lying in wait for him.

When the Justice guy raised his hand to the control lever, the sniper shot him through the front of the bus. He was using AP rounds. The strike-team man managed to hit the lever anyway, and the door opened and the kids and the wounded man were whisked away in the armored truck.

To show his displeasure, the sniper threw a woman out of the tower. She was very much alive, and screaming, until she, too, hit the stone stairs.

The SAC on the ground decided against using the armored car to rescue other people trapped in the sniper's field of fire. He figured that if they waited until dark, they could slip away without danger. Brognola agreed with the decision. Because of the terrain, the SAC was unable to deploy the countersniper teams he'd brought along. The tower was taller than any structure within a mile, which made for a bad shooting angle. Add to that the bags of cement and the hostages inside, and a countersniper response was out of the question.

At this point it was a standoff.

The armored car was still rolling up and down the streets. Federal officers with bullhorns were telling people to stay inside their houses, and to keep low and away from windows.

The dead lay where they had fallen.

Brognola knew he wasn't responsible for the situation. It was a nightmare infinitely worse than anything he had ever imagined. Short of going public, of sacrificing his career and the chance for doing good in the future, he couldn't have done more to avoid it.

He already had White House clearance to use an outside team to end the stalemate. No credentials would be presented in Bel Vista, no names exchanged. The Justice people on the ground would recognize the specialists by their helicopter ID numbers.

A phone rang, and Price answered it. She listened for a moment, then covered the mouthpiece with her hand. "It's Grimaldi on the scrambler," she said. "He says they're twenty-five miles east of Ocala. The mission was an unqualified success."

"That's great news," Brognola said. "Have him put the big guy on the line."

"We don't have to give this guy what he wants," Price said, still holding her hand over the mouthpiece. "We don't have to let him engage Striker. We can let the Army handle it."

"Trust me, what he's about to get from Striker is nothing he wants. Now, give me the phone."

22

The Justice Department helicopter buzzing around the tower annoyed Tacho Ruiz.

"Do you hear that?" he said to the remaining hostages. "It's your government out there, protecting you. Doesn't that sound make you feel safer?"

The mayor and the two workmen, their wrists wrapped tightly with tape, sat on the floor of the bell tower. There was no longer a bell suspended from the rafters overhead; it had been replaced in the early eighties by an electronic sound system, a bell on tape. At gunpoint the hostages had piled up cement bags in front of the window openings and on top of the trapdoor that led down to the stairs. The three bound men said nothing, did nothing. Their expressions were blank. They were afraid of dying. And Tacho knew they had good reason to be.

He intended to kill them all, one way or another, before the day was through.

The helicopter swooped closer, circling. It was like a big, lazy fly that was just begging to be swatted, and he had the swatter.

"See this?" he said, holding up one of the .308 cartridges he had stolen from the gun store below. "Do you know what it is?"

The mayor glared at him. The workmen refused to even look up from the floor.

"It's an M-61 armor-piercing round," he told them.

"It's made by your government's military. It will shoot through five-eights of an inch of steel at one hundred yards. It costs about two dollars. Watch what I can do with it."

He dropped the H&K's magazine, cleared the chamber of the live round that was in it, then loaded the AP cartridge into the mag. He slapped the clip back in place and released the bolt, chambering the bullet.

Tacho took a position behind one of the louvered panels, resting the MSG-90 on a bag of cement. The helicopter continued to circle, two hundred yards out. He lined up his shot and waited for the aircraft to fly into his cross hairs. The gun bucked and a spent casing flipped onto the wooden floor, joining a couple of dozen others that littered it.

The Salvadoran jumped up from the gun and followed the helicopter around the tower, peering through the slats, trying to see what he'd hit. When the chopper appeared in front of the unblocked window, it was wobbling badly from side to side.

"I nailed that *puta* of a pilot," Tacho said, looking through the binoculars hanging from a strap around his neck. "That piece of junk is going down."

"Shit," the mayor swore.

Tacho stared at the tall, skinny man. It was stupid to try to impress a paper-pusher, a politician, with trick shots. He knew Gaspar would've been impressed, though. His twin brother would've laughed out loud to see the copilot fighting to clear the controls of the dead man's body, even as the machine dropped out of the sky.

If Gaspar was laughing now, it was from the far side of hell.

Of course, there was someone else who would appreciate the kill shot he had just made. Blue Eyes.

The murders were a challenge broadcast by every TV station in the country. Tacho didn't know the North American, but he had known men just like him in El Salvador and Colombia, men who thought of themselves as honorable and decent. None of them would let a challenge like this go unanswered.

Blue Eyes was coming. He might already be out there.

That was fine with Tacho. He didn't plan on living to see another sunrise. Without his brother, life had no meaning. He would join Gaspar in hell very soon, but before he did, he would send the North American to break trail for him.

BOLAN LISTENED CAREFULLY to what Brognola had to say. As he received the information, there was no change in his facial expression, except for a slight tightening along the jawline. He immediately relayed the course change to Grimaldi, who turned south and increased speed to redline.

The followup questions the Executioner asked the head Fed were simple and straightforward, dealing with distances and logistics. They had everything they needed on board the aircraft; there was never a doubt that he would take on the job.

After Bolan broke the connection, he briefed Hawkins and Grimaldi about the situation on the ground. He made no mention of the personal angle, the note written in blood, because it was irrelevant to the completion of the mission. There were no "reasons" for killing innocent people, for using their severed body parts to daub letters on a concrete wall. For the murder of innocents, for that kind of evil, there were only rationalizations and ravings.

The Executioner didn't need to explain the taking of a murderer's life. He never had, and he never would.

When they were within five miles of Bel Vista, local air-traffic control contacted Grimaldi, warning him off.

"The Salvadoran just shot down a Justice surveillance chopper," Grimaldi told Bolan and Hawkins. "They don't want us flying anywhere near the town center."

"No problem," Bolan said. "Our LZ is a mile to the west." He pointed to their left, at a tall, silver structure that gleamed in the distance. "We'll set down beside the water tower."

As they approached the huge storage tank, they could see a police car and a black Justice van parked next to the tower's four legs. Grimaldi swooped down and landed 150 feet from the tower.

A short, stout man in a police uniform and bill cap hurried up to greet them. "Damn, we're glad you're finally here," he said, leaning into the doorway. "I'm Bill Howard, police chief of Bel Vista. We've got a hell of a mess on our hands." He looked at the gear bags on the flight deck. "Can I help you carry anything?"

"No, thanks," Bolan said. "We can manage."

As the tall man got out of the aircraft, the police chief tried to see the eyes behind the sunglasses. He couldn't help himself. He wanted to take the measure of the guy. He had seen killers before, but they had all been criminals and crazies. This man did it for the white hats. He did what every beat cop in the country at some time wished he or she could do. The police chief got a glimpse of something behind the tinted lenses; at the time, he wasn't sure what. Later, when he had the chance to think about it, he would remember it as ice-cold resolve.

The communications coordinator from the Justice van joined them at the foot of the water tank. "The situation in the tower is unchanged," he said. "You have a green light whenever you acquire the target. Everyone else is on stand-down until further notice."

Bolan took the AMAC from its case and slipped his arm through the shoulder sling.

"That's one mean-looking field piece," Howard commented.

Hawkins followed the Executioner up the steel ladder

that ran along the outside of the tower leg. He carried the astronomical spotting telescope, a pair of rolled-up foam mats and a knapsack with a selection of .50-caliber ammunition, as well as several sandbags.

It was a five-hundred-foot climb to the steel grating that formed a circular deck around the base of the water tower's silver tank. Bolan stared at the town and the spike of tower fifteen hundred yards away. The sun was to their back, the platform was rock steady and there was no wind. All he needed was luck.

Hawkins helped him set up the gun and then the spotting scope. They had a straight-on view of the right side of the tower, facing a window opening blocked by wooden louvers.

Bolan clicked in the range and found the window in his Ultra's view field. He could see the slits of the louvers as dark stripes, but the magnification wasn't enough to let him see into the tower.

Hawkins, with a higher-power instrument, could actually make out movement behind the panel. "Somebody's walking back and forth, Striker," he said. "I make the top of a head—two, four, six, eight, ten slats from the bottom."

Bolan found the mark with his cross hairs and dropped the aim point to coincide with the standard, center-chest height of a standing man. "Can you verify it's the target?"

"Negative. He's standing too far away from the louvers."

The Executioner opened the sandbagged AMAC's bolt and inserted a 700-grain hollowpoint round. He locked the bolt down on the round and scooted up into firing position on the foam mat. The scope hadn't moved an eyelash. It was zeroed at heart height in the middle of the louvered panel.

"Still no verification, Striker," Hawkins said. "No, wait! He's stepping up, right in the center of the window.

I've got skin tones. Aw, shit! Shit! The slats are in the way. I can't see enough of his face to be sure who the hell he is.''

Bolan found the AMAC's trigger with the pad of his index finger. He wasn't looking through the scope. He didn't have to.

"Can you see the teeth?" he asked.

As TIME PASSED and nothing happened, Tacho started to get anxious. He began to pace. What if Blue Eyes didn't come, after all? Then all this would have been for nothing. No, he wouldn't let himself think that. He had had a wonderful day of shooting. He had lost track of the number of people he had killed. He would go out a celebrity, a shining example of Atlacatl manliness.

"I'm going to kill you next," Tacho told the mayor of Bel Vista. "I'm going to tie a rope around your neck and throw you out the window."

Tacho stepped into the warm sunlight filtering through the window slats and smiled. "You'll be the first American politician to hang on national TV."

"IT'S HIM!" Hawkins said. "He's dead center! You've got the green!"

The Executioner tightened down with his fingertip until he felt the tension of the breakpoint come up. He increased the pressure until the sear snapped and the big gun boomed. The report echoed like thunder over the gently rolling landscape.

TACHO TURNED to face the mayor. As he did so, the wood panel beside him exploded, splinters and blood spraying over the faces of the hostages.

The Salvadoran was thrown to his knees by the impact. For an instant he didn't understand what had happened to him. He knew only that it felt like his arm had been torn out of the socket.

When he looked at himself, he couldn't believe his eyes. He had no right hand.

Protruding from his wrist was raw, red bone. The shock of the bullet was so powerful that it sealed the wound, cauterizing the vessels.

Tacho rose to his feet, clutching his forearm. Without a right hand, he couldn't shoot the H&K.

Growling a curse, the mayor leaped from the floor, his arms still bound behind his back. He drove his head into Tacho's stomach, sending him hurtling backward toward the open window. The Salvadoran tried to catch hold of something, anything as the ledge hit the backs of his legs, as he started to tumble over and out. His one good hand wasn't enough.

Tacho fell out of the tower, flailing his arms and legs. He just missed the body of the secretary he had murdered and landed face first on the stone steps. Shards of his teeth skittered down the stairs and into the street.

"Did you get him?" the police chief asked as Bolan and Hawkins stepped down from the ladder. "Did you get him?"

Neither man answered. They didn't even slow down as they walked by.

"Yeah, they got him," the communications coordinator from Justice said. "The hostages are free."

"Finally," the chief said, taking off his bill cap to mop his brow. He watched as the two specialists lugged their gear back to the waiting helicopter and climbed in. "Strange men, aren't they?"

"Very strange," the comm officer agreed.

As the helicopter rose in the air and wheeled away to the north, the chief added, "Thank God for them."

**The Stony Man commandos deliver hard justice
to a dispenser of death**

STONY MAN™ 33

PUNITIVE MEASURES

The Eliminator—a cheaply made yet effective handgun
that's being mass-produced and distributed underground—
is turning up in the hands of street gangs and criminals
throughout the world. As the grisly death toll rises, the
Stony Man teams mount an international dragnet against a
mastermind who knows that death is cheap. Now he's
about to discover that Stony Man gives retribution
away—free.

Available in February 1998 at your favorite retail outlet.

James Axler

OUTLANDERS™

OMEGA PATH

A dark and unfathomable power governs post-nuclear America. As a former warrior of the secretive regime, Kane races to expose the blueprint of a power that's immeasurably evil, with the aid of fellow outcasts Brigid Baptiste and Grant. In a pre-apocalyptic New York City, hope lies in their ability to reach one young man who can perhaps alter the future....

Nothing is as it seems. Not even the invincible past....

Available February 1998,
wherever Gold Eagle books are sold.

**A violent struggle for survival
in a post-holocaust world**

JAMES AXLER

DEATHLANDS®

Freedom Lost

Following up rumors of trouble on his old home ground, Ryan and his band seek shelter inside the walls of what was once the largest shopping mall in the Carolinas. The baron of the fortress gives them no choice but to join his security detail. As outside invaders step up their raids on the mall, Ryan must battle both sides for a chance to save their lives.

Available in March 1998 at your favorite retail outlet. Or order your copy now by sending your name, address, zip or postal code, along with a check or money order (please do not send cash) for $5.50 for each book ordered ($6.50 in Canada), plus 75¢ postage and handling ($1.00 in Canada), payable to Gold Eagle Books, to:

In the U.S.	In Canada
Gold Eagle Books	Gold Eagle Books
3010 Walden Ave.	P.O. Box 636
P.O. Box 9077	Fort Erie, Ontario
Buffalo, NY 14269-9077	L2A 5X3

Please specify book title with order.
Canadian residents add applicable federal and provincial taxes.

GOLD
EAGLE ®

GDL41